Gnomeling:
The Tales of Christian Tompta, Book 1

Gnomeling
The Tales of Christian Tompta, Book 1

Written and Illustrated
by
Dawn M. Paul

Andehem Publishing, LLC
Xenia, Ohio

ANDEHEM
PUBLISHING,
LLC

Published by Andehem Publishing, LLC.

Fiction, Juvenile Fiction, Fantasy, Adventure, Gnomes,
Magic, Coming of Age, Family Friendly

ISBN-10: 1-946813-00-1
ISBN-13: 978-1-946813-00-8

CONTENTS

FOR THE ADVENTURERS AT HEART

Thank you to my family and friends who support me, to my writing pal, Val, who edits and proofreads for me, and to my writing group friends. Special thanks to my three test readers: Lily, Spencer and Nik (and moms!).

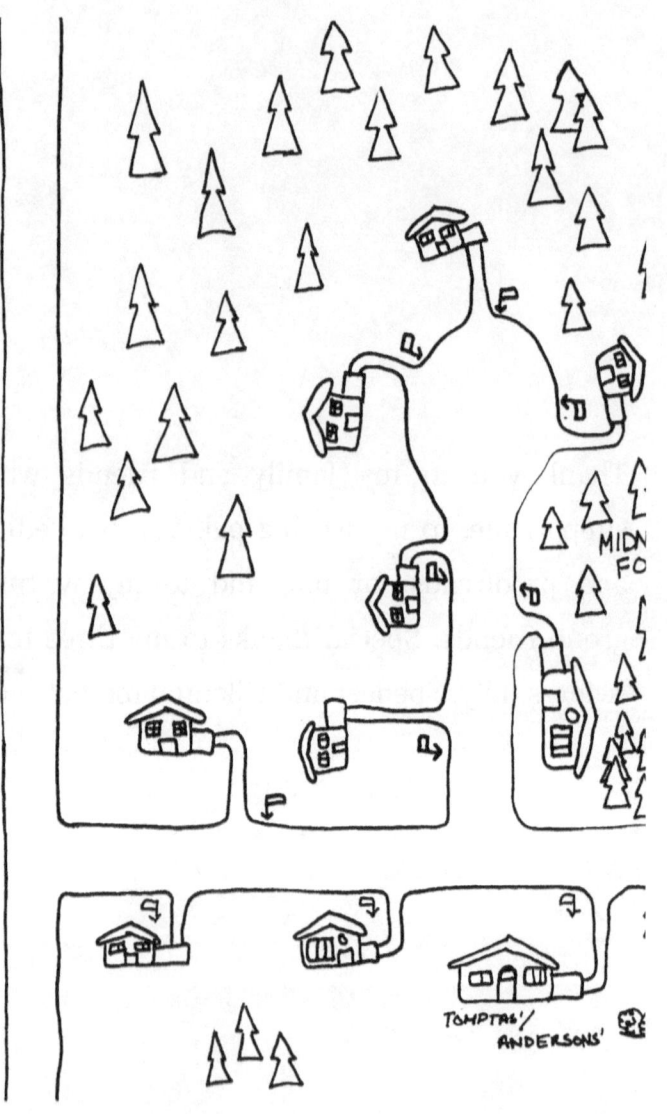

MIDN
FO

TOMPTAS'/
ANDERSONS'

MYSTIC
FOUNTAIN

NIGHT
FOREST

COBBLER

JODDEBURG
VILLAGE

OLD
SHACK

LAKE

BEEZLEYS'/OLSONS'

THE GNOME SAGA

Eons ago, when the earth was first born,
the Great Artistic Master
became lonely and mourned.
He created a race called the Barakiel,
who looked like the Master,
but clashed too much steel.
He created again, a spirit essence called Pith -
individual entities of love,
with one consciousness.
Sadly, not able to hug these bodies of mist
He conceived human beings,
and gave them a wondrous gift.
In each He turned on a faucet of creativity
Empowering the humans
to share and spread beauty.
Made from clay, they hunted,

gathered, toiled and tilled

reproducing and spreading,

but through envy, lost His good will.

The humans grew bored

and soon began to fight.

The Artistic Master grew angry

and prepared to throw down a strike.

But then He saw a painter singing,

with brushes in hand,

and the Great Master stilled for a moment,

looking over the land.

He decided the humans

had redeeming qualities,

not all of them acted in temper;

some helped others freely.

So instead of pelting down

upon these clay creatures,

He created small helpmates

with protective features.

He called them gnomes

and now they must stay hidden,

for revealing themselves to humans

became strictly forbidden.

Gnomes eat no meat

and are born from tulip flowers.

To assist in their duties,
the Master gave them magical powers.
Gnomes learn to resize objects
and then how to stiffen
into statuesque figures,
like a gargoyle or griffin.
Each gnome has a unique third power
which determines his mystical shoes
and conical hat color.
He'll earn these after he
completes a successful quest,
then the gnome will journey
to see the Cobbler,
deep in the forest.
Humans only see them as statue-like beings,
gnomes either shift to rigid mode,
or take off fleeing.
But no matter the circumstance
gnomes find themselves in
they help out their humans –
assist, guard and treat them like kin.

CHAPTER 1

"Oh thistle-stickers!" Christian said, flopping onto his bed, which squeaked loudly in protest. Earlier in the day, the young gnome had been practicing his magical ability to resize inanimate objects, but the bed did not return back to its original size and was now too short for his body. He lay back onto his pillow and propped his feet upon the footboard.

"Don't worry," said Magda, his sister, slapping her hands over her slightly pointed ears. "You'll be leaving on your mission soon..."

Christian scowled at her. *She came in here too quietly and without my permission again, the nosy nettle. Why can't she leave me alone? Just because*

9

our rooms face each other at the top of the stairs does not give her the right to sneak in whenever she feels like it! I never go in her room. It's too boring. There's nothing in there except dumb she-gnome stuff.

"...you should get lots of time to practice your magic while you're on your journey. Then, when you complete your mission, you'll become Zach's guardian, and by all the pine needles of the north, he sure needs one! It'll be your dream come true."

He looked longingly out his bedroom window, to the large books that lined the shelf, trying to ignore her. *Maybe if I don't pay attention to her she'll go away.*

The ceramic house he lived in with his family sat on the Anderson family's bookshelf and looked like a colorful mushroom. The bright orange faded to light yellow at the bottom. The ceramic artist had designed it to show bits of brick through parts of torn away mushroom skin and had splattered the walls with blue and white flowers. Smaller mushrooms and boulders lined the bottom edge. The front door looked like it was made from wood and had a stone arch surrounding it. One would never guess how big it was on the inside from the looks of the outside.

Christian's mind drifted away from his sister's voice again. *It sure is convenient to live by the books, especially since reading is all we ever get to do. Everything interesting is outside of this house!*

Christian sighed. He longed for adventure. Some days he would pretend to steer a mighty pirate ship, while other days he would practice his swordplay, using a yarn needle as a sword and a button his father had brought home as a shield. The human books he picked out to read were full of action and contained many exploits that seemed both fun and daring. *I just know I could easily overcome any obstacle that arose in one of those stories, just like the heroes in the books...*

"I can't wait to get my shoes. And the conical hat!" Magda said excitedly, pulling Christian from his daydream. He scowled at first, then smiled and stared dreamily at the ceiling, considering her words. He stretched, putting his hands under his head. Immediately he felt his knitted cap.

"This beanie makes me look like a baby!" He yanked the cap off of his head and threw it across the room. It hit a cup of water on the table, causing it to wobble precariously. Only a few drops splashed out before the cup settled back down to its original position.

"Has Mama or Papa told you yet what you have to do?" Magda swiped at the water drops with her sleeve and picked up the beanie before sitting down on the floor cross-legged. She took apart and reworked the braid that draped from the top of the cap.

"No, but it would be cool to catch pirates, or maybe bring down some gangsters, or even save a princess. Well, you know, not a *real* princess, but a someone in distress."

Christian glanced quickly at Magda.

She rolled her eyes at him. "You've been reading

too many books. They would never give you those kinds of jobs. They're too dangerous and you're only twelve," Magda said, in her know-it-all voice.

Christian sat up abruptly and shot her the stink eye. "I'll be thirteen in the spring! And...and..." he sputtered, "...they trust me."

Magda shook her head slowly, playing with the strings in her hand. ""Yeah, but you know what I mean. You're too young to catch grown-ups. I heard Papa tell Mama that it took four grown gnomes to stop one human teen who was painting on a building!" She shook her head again. "His guardian really needed help to keep him out of trouble."

"When you stop to think about it, it's strange that folk our size could catch a giant human," said Christian, "even if it's not fully grown." *Oh, I can't wait to be a guardian! But why would a human get in trouble for painting? I am NOT going to ask her. I wonder if that could happen to me, with my drawings. Well, I'll never paint on any buildings.*

"I know, right? I don't know how they did it without being seen, but they did. They must've used a net or something, but it probably helped having four gnomes against one teenager." She lifted her face and set down the cap. "I wonder what would have happened to the gnomes if they were seen? They would have broken our strongest gnome law! That would've been so bad..." She shuddered as she pulled at the cap, trying to shape it.

Christian watched her for a moment before she threw it at his head. She missed. It landed on the floor next to his feet.

Then she said quietly, "Anyway, I'll miss you while you're gone. And I'll worry about you because it'll only be your third time outside - ever!" She sniffed and swiped at her face as she stood up, staring at the floor.

He picked up the cap and tossed it onto his nightstand, releasing a sigh. *She's right. My lack of experience is going to be a problem... Hmm... I'm not going to focus on that right now.*

His focus returned to Magda. "Oh, just read. All these books will keep your mind off me," he said, waving his hand toward the window. "Speaking of books, you'd better resize that *Alice in Wonderland* book and put it back. Hope was looking for it the other day."

Magda glanced out the window of their little house, toward the books squeezed tightly together on the shelf.

Sadness turned to frustration as Christian added gruffly, "And stay out of my room while I'm gone, Nosy Nettle!"

Magda's stormy eyes turned up swiftly toward her brother as she put both hands on her hips and stamped a foot. "Don't call me that! My name is Magda!"

Christian chuckled. "Why not? You're nosy and annoying like nettle, Nettle."

"Ugh! Maybe you won't even succeed in your mission! Have you thought about that? Huh? Have you?" Magda stamped her foot again, shook her fists at Christian and turned toward the door. They both paused a moment just then, as their mother called them to dinner.

Magda turned back and stuck her tongue out at him before stomping out. He heard her thumping steps all the way down the stairs. Christian frowned. *What will I do if I fail? I won't be able to be Zach's guardian, and it's all I've ever wanted to do. I'll probably get sent to guard chickens somewhere or something else dumb. Oh, weeds and twigs!*

He dragged himself up from his bed and slowly made his way down the stairs.

CHAPTER 2

By the time Christian reached the bottom of the steps, his shoulders slumped and his head hung low. Fear of the unknown was getting the better of him.

"Sit ya down, Mags. Come sit down, Tanny."

I wish she wouldn't call me that. I'm getting too old for a nickname.

His mother bustled around the table as she spooned food into bowls. Hearing his mother's accented voice caused a warmth to blossom in Christian's chest and soothed him. "Yer Papa tought he might be late and told me ta go ahead and feed ya gnomelings."

Christian noticed the new pan and ladle she was

holding. It suddenly occurred to him that she must have shrunken them from human size. Having been practicing so hard on his own resizing power, he looked around at the tidy kitchen and admired her skill. It closely resembled the enormous humans' kitchen and he wondered if she had to shrink everything herself. Maybe Papa had helped, or she had found the items another way...

Shaking himself to regain focus, Christian asked, "Mama, did your family have to go on missions to earn their mystical shoes and conicals back before they migrated here from Minnesota?"

"Vy, of course dey did, Tanny!"

"When are you and Papa going to tell me what my mission will be?" His voice cracked as he studied his bowl and picked at a spot on the wooden table. Normally he would rush to shovel food into his mouth, but thoughts of his mission made him feel a little queasy.

"Vell, Tanny, yer fadder vas going ta talk ta ya about dat tanight."

"Really?" he yelped, raising his eyebrows and sitting up straighter in his chair.

"Mama, Christian thinks he is going to go catch criminals!" Magda said, and then she laughed at him. Her spoon reflexively banged on the table - which made her snort.

"Oh, fer veeds and tvigs," his mother said, trying hard to smother her chuckle as the ladle shook in her hand. When she straightened up from filling her own bowl, the ladle slipped from her hand and clattered to the floor. She guffawed loudly and slapped her leg before turning to her son.

"Dough ya're a special boy, Christian Martin Tompta, don't go tinking ya're up fer a job like dat, now!" She wheezed. "It takes many strong gnomes vit da help of der Pit partners ta go catching big-time criminals. Yer fadder just told me it took four of his cousins ta get dat little vipper-snapper painter last veek!"

Bewildered by his mother's laughter, Christian waited for her to calm down. *What is so funny?*

After a few moments she caught her breath, but continued to smile at him as she ruffled his hair and then picked up the ladle. Magda held her hands over her mouth and nose as she snickered at Christian. He gave her the stink eye.

"Now vat are ya snickering at, Magda Matilda Tompta? Dat teenage human vas a menace. He spray-painted some pretty nice brick valls down da road. Vat do ya tink he vould do dat fer? He ruined a perfectly nice place fer no good reason." Magda looked down, abashed.

"Mama?" Christian caught her attention. "Why'd a painter get in trouble?" he asked, then slurped a spoonful of the steaming soup.

"Did ya even hear a vord I just said?" She shook her head and grumbled, "Just eat yer soup." She set the ladle inside the pan and put both on the candle pot heater.

"But..." he began, then Magda kicked him under the table and stuck out her tongue at him.

"Ow!" He rubbed his leg.

When their mother returned to the table she said again, "Ya know, dose poor human darlings, Hope and Zach, aren't as hardy and healty as ve gnome folk! Vy, it vasn't but vat, two monts ago now, dat young Hope had dat nasty cough..."

Christian made sure to slurp loudly so that his mother heard him eating his soup and would know he was listening to her.

"...Ya gnomelings haven't been sick since ya vere just little ones. Ve all caught dat Flower Lily sneeze. Vat a mess dat made, flying pollen and sneezing spittle everyvere. I had ta dust, vipe and vash all hours of da day. And I had ta vear dat old nasty scarf tied over my face. I vas very glad, I tell ya, ven ve passed trough dat. Yer Uncle Rupert vas lucky he didn't catch it, but I'd bet it's cause he chews on dat old stinky pipe. Da stink must have frightened da lily dust avay." She laughed at her own joke. "Oh! Dere's yer Papa now."

Christian's father's high-pitched whistling floated through the window into the kitchen, which was a sign he was climbing onto their shelf. The whistling stopped abruptly when his father called out, "How goes there, Rupert?"

Christian's hand stilled in midair as he watched his mother glide toward the front door.

"Oh, same as usual, I suppose," his uncle said. "Nothin' jumped from the books today." Uncle Rupert chuckled.

Christian looked at his sister and they both giggled.

"Hallo there, Zelma!" his father crooned, as the door opened. "How's my lovely wife this evening?" He leaned over, kissed her cheek, and then removed his orange conical and handed it to her. She set his pointy hat on the gold-trimmed wooden shelf, next to her red one. Christian stared at the conicals, imagining his future hat lined up alongside them, in the place of honor.

Christian's father took off his jacket and hung it on a peg under the shelf. Next, he carefully pushed off first one glittering orange shoe and then the other, putting them into their place on a mat under his jacket. Christian studied the shiny pairs lined up next to each other. *Will mine be orange like Papa's, or perhaps red like Mama's? Or maybe another color altogether? It all depends on what my third power will be, but I sure wish it would come already!*

"Vy, I'm better dan spring flowers!" his mother said, bustling to fill the last empty bowl. The ladle banged the pot, snapping Christian from his daydream. "Sit ya down here, Klaus. I've made a lovely parsley dumpling soup fer dinner. It'll feel good in yer belly."

"Mmmhmm..." His father's big nose sniffed the air. "It smells delightful. Hello, my gnomelings!" His smile beamed around the room.

"Hi, Papa!" said Magda, jumping up to hug her father. She quickly squeezed around his big belly and then hopped back onto her seat.

"Hi, Papa..." said Christian, quietly, while

picking at that spot on the table.

"Whoa ho there, Tanny; what's your trouble? You'd best be careful, or you'll get a splinter."

"He can't wait for his mission, Papa!" Magda tucked her hands into her pockets and bounced her feet up and down under the table. "Mama said you were going to tell him what it is tonight!"

Christian gave her the stink eye before looking back down at his soup. He picked up his spoon again and pushed dumplings around in the bowl.

His father boomed, "Is this true, Son? Have you got the ants in your pants?"

Christian looked up at his father, saw him smile and wink, and then giggled. "Oh, Papa, you know there are no ants in my pants!"

His father's smile broadened further, and he chuckled. "I guess you're right, Tanny. After dinner we will sit down with a nice cake..." he looked to Mama who nodded, "...and strawberry tea to discuss your mission before we read."

Conversation buzzed around Christian while he ate, but he could not focus. *What could it be? I wonder if I'll go outside. That's pretty scary, there are so many dangerous wild animals and human contraptions. But it sounds exciting! Oooo, what would I see out there? Or maybe I'll go into the back of the house to do something. Maybe I'll finally get to see Zach's room! Oh, what else could it be?*

When his spoon clacked the empty bottom of his bowl, he looked up and caught his mother winking at his sister, and then they both stared at him. Swallowing his last bit of dumpling, he dropped his spoon into the bowl, began tapping his thumbs on the table and asked, "What?"

"Please sit still, you two. I cannot enjoy this fine soup Mama made while you're all wiggly squiggly!" Both children settled for a few moments, but then resumed their tapping and fidgeting while they waited for their parents to finish their dinner. After dropping her spoon into her bowl, his mother folded her hands together and studied him with a furrowed brow.

"Tanny, did I see ya finish yer book last night?"

"Yes, Mama." He watched his father tip his bowl to slurp out the remains of his soup.

"And how are ya coming along on yers, Mags?" Magda tipped her bowl to finish the last of her soup, copying Papa.

"I'm almost done, Mama," she said, hopping off

her chair.

His mother looked from one child's bowl to the other's and then nodded. "Go ahead. Clear yer dishes."

"The cowboy, the cowgirl and the space guy just jumped on the pony's back to get away when I had to quit last night!" Christian looked at Magda. She sounded excited. *That must've been a good book.*

"Ya'd better go get a new book, Christian, and take yer sister vit ya. She'll finish her story quickly tanight." Christian sighed, nodded and looked at his sister. He felt slightly tender toward Magda for just a moment, secretly acknowledging that nobody wanted to be left empty-handed, with nothing to read.

They brought their dishes to the sink. Magda went to grab the *Alice in Wonderland* book and met Christian at the door. Just as Magda reached for the handle, his mother startled both of them when she cried, "Oh! Look first, my gnomelings! Be careful no humans are about. And remember ta treat da books wit respect, fer dey are not ours. Ve only borrow dem. Vords are valuable-ve don't vant ta lose or damage dem."

Magda instantly dropped her hand from the

door handle. She carefully lifted the peephole cover, and then she opened the door. Christian shook his head and followed her out onto the bookshelf. *She should know better by now.*

He quietly pulled the door closed behind them.

"Hi, Uncle Rupert!" Magda called, waving to the gnome nestled in a corner on the next bookcase over. He sat still, with a pipe in one hand and a book across his lap.

"Shhhh, child!" he said sternly, before pointing his thumb toward the front hallway. Christian watched his uncle's face harden and turn shiny as he went into rigid mode. Christian's eyes followed the direction of the thumb to see Zach, the human, stepping through the front door.

CHAPTER 3

Christian's breath whooshed from his chest and he immediately shifted into rigid mode, stiffening like a statue. He glanced at Magda, whose skin looked like a smooth shiny rock, and then let out a slow breath, relieved that she had already stiffened.

Christian envied Magda's quickness with her magic. He did not understand how at two years younger than him, she was already better at stiffening faster than him. She always won when they competed, but he sometimes bested her in their resizing competitions. *Even if she is annoying, I still don't want her to get caught by a human!*

Christian watched Zach slip off his shoes. The boy had those black round things over his ears again, though they blended in with his short brown curly hair. Stuck in rigid mode for the moment, his thoughts drifted. *I wonder what those things are. He wears them every time I see him, but they don't seem warm.*

Zach hung his coat on the hall tree. *Where did he go all day? I should ask Mama since he comes and goes a lot - way more than I get to go out. That's not fair since we're almost the same age! Going outside does seem both scary and exciting, but either way when I become his guardian, I'll have to do it more often, for sure.*

Zach's sister, Hope, came stomping in the front door. She gave her brother the stink eye, and then she nudged him as she marched straight past him and out of sight. Zach stood staring after her for a moment, and then he also disappeared behind the hall wall and out of Christian's sight. Christian stayed in rigid mode as he listened to the boy's footsteps retreat toward the back of the house. *Zach's probably going back to his own room. Oh, rose spurs, I wish I could go see it! My parents hardly ever let me do anything!*

When he heard a distant door shut, Christian let out a long breath and relaxed, loosely shaking his limbs. Luckily Zach had not seen them, but they did not have much time before the Anderson parents came home.

"Come on, Magda, let's get our books."

Christian watched her face turn from shiny and glazed back to normal as she unstiffened, shaking her arms and dropping the book. She looked at Christian thoughtfully for a moment, but did not say anything before she turned and jump-climbed to the top shelf, where the children's books were kept.

Christian and his sister loved to look at the human books - they were so tall. The gnomelings would stand with their backs to books and measure their growth against them. Sometimes during the day, when the human family was gone, they would sit on the edge of the bookshelf and dangle their feet off as they read, trying not to get caught by their mother.

They would laugh when they resized the books a little too big. Sometimes, if they tried to hold them on their laps to read them in the bigger size, the books would often fall of their own accord, all the way down to the floor. The gnomelings then would have to drop-climb down to get them and jump-climb back up to their shelf. Christian liked to get out of their little home and away from their studies, which were all about plants, animals and gnome history.

He thought back to Zach. *It's not as fun picking out books when we almost get caught!*

Christian drop-climbed down a shelf and picked up the book that Zach had tossed onto it the day before. On the cover, a man looked back over his shoulder while running through a city. *This looks like it has lots of action. I'll try it.*

He closed his eyes and put the tips of his fingers together, placing his pointer fingers on the bridge of his nose and placing his thumbs under his chin.

He concentrated hard on making the books gnome-sized and blew into his palms. As the breath whizzed through his hands, he spread the backs of his hands apart to aim the air at the book. The air above the book shimmered a bit as light hit dust particles, and the book began to shrink.

Perfect. I can do books with no problem, so why do I have such trouble with my bed?

"I'm done."

Christian jerked, startled. He bristled as he looked up at Magda's head, which hung down from the shelf above. Panic rose quickly inside him as he realized he had not heard her climb back down while in the midst of working his magic. *That could be dangerous. I need to pay closer attention.*

He waved at her to back up. Then he tossed his book up to her, before jump-climbing up the shelf.

"Why did you pick out that baby book?" Christian asked her, frustrated that she had caught him unaware.

"I like the rhymes," she said, and then she stuck her tongue out at him. It made him laugh, and he shook his head, quickly forgiving her, because his shock was not her fault.

"Come on," he said, letting out a sigh.

They waved to their uncle, who still sat in the same spot reading, though not in rigid mode. He lifted his pipe in salute and winked.

When the young gnomes returned inside, their parents were sitting in chairs around a sweet Leilani flower, planted in a large blue pot. Mama had saved a clipping from the plant that the human, Mrs. Anderson, had to give away because the odor was too strong for her.

Ahhh, home. Christian caught a whiff of the flower. For a brief moment, he envisioned Mrs. Anderson sneezing. He paused nervously at the thought, because whenever Mrs. Anderson came near the bookcase, her sneeze would cause her to search briefly for the faint scent. They always had to hide when she was near, but luckily, she had not found the small flower yet. *I hope she never does.*

Christian and his sister sat down in their own chairs, but before they could open their books, Papa spoke. "So... Tanny, you are curious about your mission, eh?"

"Yes, sir." Christian nodded. Both excited and nervous, he tapped his thumbs on his legs, "What will my mission be? What do I have to do?"

"Well, Son, in order for a gnome to become a

guardian, they must pass a test of great responsibility to show that they are able to make good decisions while helping and protecting."

Christian's hands began to quiver. He clutched his book tightly in his lap to stop the shaking.

"Mama and I have decided on a job for you, from an opportunity that arrived on our doorstep last night. A misdirected moth delivered a message to us for the Beezleys next door, by mistake."

"The Beezleys?" asked Christian, raising his eyebrow in question.

"Yes, our gnome neighbors at the humans' house across the acreage over there?" He pointed toward the back of the house.

"Oh, yeah..." He nodded, pretending to recognize whom his father meant. Papa raised his eyebrows. Christian blinked several times, and then shrugged his shoulders.

"Anyway, Mama and I have decided that it should be you, rather than Uncle Rupert or me, to deliver the message to them. We think it's the perfect mission for a gnomeling such as yourself." Christian's mouth dropped open.

"You mean... I have to cross the yard? By myself? What about all those dangers outside?" Images from the animal and insect books he had read flashed through his mind.

"Well, that's part of growing up, Tanny - learning new things and taking on more responsibility. This message needs to get to the correct address, and soon, so you'll need to leave the day after tomorrow." Papa did not smile.

Christian gulped.

"Papa, I can't wait for my mission!" Magda interrupted, bouncing in her seat. Everyone turned to look at her and Christian rolled his eyes. *Goody two-shoes!*

"Hush, Mags!" His mother admonished. "Dis is Tanny's and Papa's talk, now."

"Papa..." said Christian, drawing his father's attention back from his sister, "...what if I fail?" He intently studied his sock, picking at the fuzz. He could not look at his father.

"I have faith in you, Christian," said Papa softly. Christian looked up at him. "I have watched you grow into a fine young gnome. Even though you have a temper sometimes, you tend to make good choices - like being patient with your sister while picking out new books this evening." Christian smiled at his father, and then turned to stare at

Magda intensely. She looked down at her fidgety fingers. *I hope she's thinking about how we were almost spotted earlier. I wonder if Papa knows how close a call we had.*

He turned back toward his father, shook his head and forced himself to refocus on the conversation.

"Papa, if the message is really important, why don't I go tomorrow?"

"You need a day to prepare and pack, and I need to go over a few things with you before you leave."

"Pack? How long will that take me? What will I need to pack?"

Both his parents chuckled, and then Papa said, "You'll probably be gone about a week, but if you aren't back then, Uncle Rupert and I will come find you."

"A week?" Christian exclaimed, blinking his wide round eyes. He swiped at the hair that kept catching in his eyelashes.

"'Tis much furder dan it looks," said his mother, opening her book. "Now, dat's enough discussing fer tanight. Let's get a little reading in before ve go ta bed. It'll help everyvun sleep better, and den ve vill pack ya up tamorrow."

They all settled in to read, but Christian could not focus on his book as thoughts roiled around in his head. *Why will the journey take so long? Will it be hard to trudge through the grass? Am I going to get lost? Why do the humans live so far apart?*

Christian gulped again. After a few minutes he asked his father, "Why do we guard humans, Papa?"

"Well, you know that the Master Artist created the humans with the greatest gift: the gift of creativity." At Christian's nod he continued, "Sometimes they use their ability in a manner that's not good for them or the earth, and it causes many problems. It is our job to watch over and help them – secretly, of course."

"Doesn't sound like they're very smart if they don't take care of the land," said Christian with a snort. "But, Papa, why us?"

"Well, now, Son, nobody is perfect...except the Master Artist. That is why he made us, to be helpers. Every human family has its own guardian. There aren't enough gnomes to cover all the humans individually, and there are jobs that need doing in our own gnome culture." His father winked at him.

"Oh yeah? Like what?"

"Well, Tanny, there are keepers of the chronicles, like your Uncle Rupert. They watch over the written word, sometimes in books and other times on scrolls or important human documents. We have gnomes to guard the trees in the forests, farm animals, forest animals, meadowlands, rivers and streams and the creatures who live in them, and the birds. Then there are gnomes who work in villages, such as the gnome council who serve and protect gnomes, the moth message service and we can't forget about mother gnomes who take care of gnomelings, like your Mama. There will be plenty of jobs to do if you aren't able to become Zach's guardian after this mission. We will find a job for you to do until you may try again - next year."

"Ok, gnomelings, dat's enough fer tanight. Time fer bed," said his mother, clapping her book closed with a huff.

CHAPTER 4

"Dis heavy fog is not good fer Christian's mission, Klaus. Dose feral cats lurk in da mist and could happen upon our little gnomeling in an instant!"

Christian overheard his mother and father talking the next morning as he slowly descended the stairs, reading a book. He stopped mid-step at her words and leaned forward to eavesdrop a little better.

"I'm a little worried too, but you know the cats will leave him alone as long as he doesn't provoke them," said his father. "It's his time, Zelma."

Christian slammed his book closed, stomped down the last few steps, and entered the kitchen. He did not want to hear anymore.

"How are ya, Tanny?" asked his mother, quickly standing to get him some breakfast. "Did ya sleep alright? Ya look tired dis morning."

Christian nodded to his father and then turned toward his mother and shook his head. "No, I didn't. Not at all. I never thought it would take me a whole week to get to the house next door and back! I had a lot to think about."

Both of his parents nodded.

"Papa has decided ta stay home taday ta talk ta ya about different situations dat might arise on yer journey, instead of going ta vork vit Mr. Anderson," his mother said, stirring a pot.

"Really, Papa? Thanks!" Christian jumped up to hug his father, and then abruptly dropped his arms and stepped back before his father could embrace him. "I mean," he cleared his throat, "thank you, Papa." Christian's face heated up.

"Why...what's that then?" his father asked, looking startled, arms hanging in midair.

Christian shuffled his feet and shrugged. "I just thought that maybe now that I'm going on this journey, I shouldn't hug all over you like a little gnomeling."

His father cleared his throat and dropped his

arms to his sides.

"You will always be my son, and I will always appreciate a good solid hug, Tanny!" His father scowled, raising a spoon to his mouth.

Christian sat down quietly to eat his porridge. His mother and father both picked up their books, so he did too. He spooned porridge into his mouth while he read. *I'm not going to finish this new book before I leave. I guess it'll be waiting for me when I get back.*

Magda bounced into the kitchen. "Are you finished with your breakfast already?" she asked, looking around the table at empty bowls.

Christian's shoulders relaxed. Nobody had spoken since the hug incident. *I'm glad she's here. I wonder if Papa's angry with me. I didn't know what to say.*

"Yes, Mags, my girl. I'm going to take Tanny on a walk around the big house this morning, just as soon as the Andersons leave."

Christian stood up and put his bowl, wooden spoon and cup near the washbasin. "Thanks for the porridge, Mama," he said, looking at her from under his lashes. He hoped she would smile at him.

"Yer velcome, Tanny," she said, nodding and

smiling kindly. "Go ahead and put on yer boots - after ya've gotten yerself ready for da day, of course. And make sure ya comb yer hair."

"Oh, Mama," sighed Christian. "I don't need to comb my hair. I'll just put on my cap."

"I need ta vash dat old smelly beanie of yers before ya leave tamorrow. I vant ya ta look yer best ven ya begin yer adventure."

"Oh, alright..." Christian shuffled around the corner and up the stairs to his room. A pitcher sat on his dresser holding stale water from the previous night. He used the dusty water to brush his teeth, spitting into a matching bowl, and then he looked at his reflection in the mirror that hung above his dresser. There were dark circles under his eyes. He pulled his eyelids up and around, and then pulled the skin underneath his eyes down, making funny faces in the mirror. He found a pimple on his cheek. *Oh thistle-stickers!* He rubbed at the ugly spot, pushing and pulling his skin one way and then another.

Backing away from the dresser, he flexed his arms to check his biceps. *I think they're getting a little bigger.*

"Come along now, Tanny!" He flinched at his

father's call. "Let's go!"

Christian ran back down the steps, slid his feet into his boots and put on his jacket.

"Ok, Papa, I'm ready!"

"I tought I told ya ta comb yer hair," said his mother. He cringed when she licked her fingers and advanced on him. He tried to back away, but she clutched his shoulder and smoothed down the hair that stood up at the back of his head.

"Oh, Zelma, leave the boy alone..." chuckled his father, shaking his head. He pulled a large mallet from a drawer in the kitchen, donned his conical, checked the peephole and stepped out the door. Christian followed closely behind him.

CHAPTER 5

"So... what are we going to do, Papa?" asked Christian as he followed his father, drop-climbing down the bookcase. At the bottom, his father stopped to wait for him.

"Once a month I walk along every wall to make sure there aren't any unwanted visitors." As he spoke, he twirled his arm around in a wide circle above his head. "All types of things can come in through the tiniest hole in the wall: mice, bats, birds, snakes and insects. We like the insects, but the humans don't, and I wouldn't want any to get hurt without a good reason. I carry a mallet just in case, but I usually am able to guide them back outside without too much trouble, or carry them if they won't budge. Occasionally a gnome is born who is able to speak to animals, but it's a rare gift. Oh, having that power would make life much easier sometimes." He turned and walked toward the wall nearest the bookcases, gesturing for Christian to follow.

"When did your third power come in, Papa?" Christian asked.

"Hmm?" His father reached the wall and began walking along the perimeter. Christian followed behind, watching him slide his hands up and down over the baseboard, checking for holes. Christian mimicked his father, running his hands up and down the walls. Back and forth he went, until his hands started to feel numb.

"When did your third power come in? I've been practicing stiffening and resizing, for a long time now, so I'm ready for something new."

"Oh, do you mean my super strength? Hmm… When I was about your age." He nodded back toward Christian and then continued, "You know that your third power is determined at birth, right? The Vulcan tulip that I was born from produces gnomes with strength that can match a human's. This helps me wield the mallet. One bounce from this will knock out whichever creature it hits, without killing it. Two knocks and the creature will die. I only had to use it once that way when I wasn't much older than you." He shivered and stared into space. "That mean gopher still haunts me."

"I wonder what mine will be."

His father stared at him for a moment, and then understanding dawned. He placed his arm around Christian's shoulders as they walked on.

Papa said, "We almost always know what a gnome's power will be, based on which tulip bears him or her. Rarely do we have an incident like what happened at your birth, when the nurse fell asleep and we found you lying in the tulip patch." They stopped. Shaking his head, he said, "I'm afraid we just can't be sure what your third power will be."

Interest turned to boredom for Christian as they resumed their investigation. Christian trailed behind his father. He followed him up over furniture and back down again. They squeezed into tight spaces where furniture corners met walls. He kept pace until he tripped and fell over a cord. *Stupid cord!*

Helping him up, Papa said, "Don't worry, Son. You'll soon know your third gift. The important thing to think about now is your mission." Then he mumbled quietly, resuming the search, "We don't want to put too much pressure on Pith for gnome business."

I don't think I was supposed to hear that.

Christian followed his father for a few minutes and then said, "Wait, Papa, is Pith real? I thought that was only a story."

"Yes, of course it... er... they are, Son. What do you think happens when you earn your mystical shoes and conical hat?"

Christian stopped in his tracks, befuddled. Scrunching his forehead, trying to remember, he said, "Well, I've heard you and Uncle Rupert talking about going into Geist, but I didn't really know what you meant. Is that where Pith lives?" At his father's nod, he continued, "So, do the shoes and conical take you there?" His father nodded again.

Christian was delighted to understood the topic better. "The way they shimmer is really cool. How do they do that?"

"If you are successful in your quest, I will take you to the Cobbler to get your own set. We will stop in the village where you can see gnomes weave a sturdy fabric from the hair of thistle seeds. The Cobbler uses that cloth to make our shoes and conicals, then he dips them in the Mystic Fountain. It's deep in the Midnight Forest."

He paused for a moment, putting a finger on his chin before resuming. "It's an odd thing, that fountain is. A tiny water spurt erupts from a steep rock face throwing water straight out, then it falls and barely makes a splash into the pond below. There's a small sandy beach where you can don your new garb. Mist glimmers in rainbow colors and it's so quiet the water scarcely makes a sound. I've only been there the one time, when I received my own conical and shoes, but tradition says it's the main portal into Geist, the spirit realm. That is why dipping our shoes and conicals in the water allows us to pass through the veil between realms."

Christian's mind had started to wander, but at that last sentence he shook his head and stopped walking. "Wait, what?"

"What, what?"

Christian asked, "Did you say we could pass through a veil?"

His father nodded.

"I don't understand," Christian shook his head. Fog was building in his brain.

"Geist is the spirit side of Earth," said his father.

"There has always been a spirit realm here in the midst of the physical realm. Beings live amongst each other in both realms, using the same, but not quite the same, space." He shook his head. "It's hard to explain."

Excitement grew in Christian. "You mean... We're not alone?" He looked all around his body, at the floor, the ceiling and throughout the room. "Do I have a Pith standing next to me?"

"No." His father chuckled. "Even though we gnomes are made from the mud of this earth, the Master decided we would serve better as guardians if we had access to both realms. We need to wear our mystical shoes and conicals to pass through, though. Hmm...that fountain really is quite a strange sight, right there in the middle of the forest."

As Christian thought on the things his father had told him about, his hands began to sweat and his stomach fluttered. So much information overwhelmed him. Before long, he took a deep breath, and focused his mind and hands back on checking walls as he and his father continued around the inside perimeter of the house.

Christian needed to focus. He practiced his

resizing power when it became necessary to hide their footprints in the dusty spots behind shelving units. First, he made the dust grow, and then he waved his arms around to stir it up, and then he shrunk it again and let if fall in a natural pattern.

"You know, Tanny, I also delivered a message for my mission."

"How did you do, Papa? On your mission, I mean."

"I succeeded, Son. It was hairy scary for a while, and that's all I'll say for now. I don't want you to be frightened, but the trials we gnomes face are meant to build character, courage, virtue and responsibility." He nodded with a serious expression. "That is why they are difficult."

Christian stopped to look around at the many rooms they had covered. *No wonder my legs are sore.*

"Well, Son, all is in order today. It's time to go pack for your journey."

"How come we didn't go down that hallway back there?" He gestured with his thumb over his shoulder.

"There wasn't enough time. I will take care of the back of the house this afternoon, and the garage as well. It's almost time for lunch now, and you know we don't want to miss a meal!"

Christian's stomach growled. He smiled and nodded. "Oh, yeah, okay. Just one more thing, Papa... What should I pack?"

His father looked at the clock on the wall and sighed, and then he sat down on the carpet, leaned against the back of the sofa facing the bookshelves, and gestured for Christian to join him. "Well, Tanny, I think you should pack as light as possible, for easy travel. You don't want extra weight to slow you down."

He put hand to chin, studying the ceiling in thought. "Now that we are into autumn, you'll need your jacket and hat in case it gets cold. You should pack a lightweight blanket for sleeping. You'll need a canteen to carry water and, of course, food. You're lucky it hasn't frosted over yet, because you'll be able to suck grass juice to get your daily nutrients, so you won't have to carry too much food. You'll still be able to fill your canteen with dew in the mornings." He smiled and patted Christian's leg. "A knife is always handy to cut and carve, and you will need to borrow my compass."

"Really?" Christian squeaked. He slapped a hand

across his mouth, cleared his throat and sat up straighter. "I mean...really?" *Papa trusts me with his compass... He really must have faith in me.*

"Yes, I've been saving it for you. Keep it safe though, because Magda may need it as well, when it's her turn for a mission. So let's see... that's a blanket, a knife, a compass, food and water. I think that'll do, Son."

"Can I go pack now?"

His father shook his head. "After lunch."

Christian nodded, jumped up and ran to the bookcase. He turned back to his father, who was also getting to his feet. "Thanks for today, Papa."

Then he clutched the bottom shelf and jump-climbed up the bookcase.

CHAPTER 6

Later that afternoon, Christian paced his room. He repeated the message his father gave him after lunch over and over out loud, trying to memorize it. Papa had made him repeat it three times, and then sent Christian upstairs to pack.

Christian put the items Papa suggested in his bag, and then he decided to pack a stack of dried daisy petals and his dye-stick in case he wanted to draw something he saw. He felt both excitement and fear at what possible adventures awaited him outside.

Mama called, "Come along now, my gnomelings!"

He raced his sister down the stairs and won. Magda elbowed him.

"Ow!" He rubbed his arm.

His mother tsked and said, "I vant ta show ya someting before ya go tamorrow, Tanny."

Christian looked at Magda; she shrugged. They followed their mother out the door and down the bookcase, through the dining room and kitchen into the laundry room. Once there, they climbed a wire-tiered shelf to look out a window.

"Dat is da house vere Mrs. Beezley lives vit her family." Mama pointed out the window to a house in the distance. "She's da von ta deliver da message ta. Dere is a vindow under da middle red-leafed bush on da side of da house, dough ya can't see it from here. Knock tree times and somevon vill let ya in. Now, ya need ta try ta make a direct pat across da grass. See dat hill, dere?"

"I can't see it!" said Magda, pushing her nose against the glass.

"Just dere, behind da big elm tree. Christian, can ya see it?"

He squinted his eyes and thought he was looking at the right place. "Yes, Mama."

"Vatch out dere cause da hill hides a small pond dat da frogs like ta visit. It's been a long time since I vas out dere, but coy fish used ta live in da pond as vell. Dey vould love da bright colors of yer clotes, so stay clear of dat. If ya get too close er fall in, day vil try ta bite ya! Now, see dat semicircle of big bushes?"

Christian turned his head slightly right. "Yes, Mama."

"Don't go near dere. It's home ta many birds, including bigger species like voodpeckers, cardinals and red-vinged black birds. Dey vill also love yer colors." She stopped speaking for a moment and Christian could almost see ideas floating above her head before she resumed, "Let's make sure yer clotes blend in vit da grass, alright? Vun a dose birds may snag da cap right off yer head!"

"Ok, Mama." Her shoulders dropped slightly as she relaxed a bit, so Christian turned back to the window.

"Now, do ya see dose rocks?" When she received no answer she said, "Christian, are ya listening ta me?" She again pointed out the window.

"Yes, Mama." Christian's gaze had fallen to a dead bug lying in the windowpane. He looked back up, out the window, though he had trouble keeping his eyes aimed where her finger pointed. His eyes betrayed him, straying back to the bug.

"Dat should be a safe place ta camp on yer second night." Christian's eyes snapped back to the window. "Von of dose rocks has a piece broken on da bottom vere ya can squveeze into, and den cover up vit yer blanket. Creatures should not be able ta see ya dere. Now, do ya understand vat I've told ya?" She looked at him with a frown and a raised eyebrow.

Christian nodded. "Yes, Mama, but where should I sleep the first night?"

"Oh, good heavens! Didn't I tell ya dat?" She chuckled. "Right here, at da end of da car pad. It looks exposed, but da car pad pops up from da ground a bit, so even dough ya von't have total cover, ya'll have some protection from da vedder. Hmm... I tink I'll make sure ta give ya da green blanket. It should blend in best vit da grass. Also, make sure ta vear yer green shirt. Vish yer old cap vas green instead of blue, but ya'll have ta make due! Now, do ya have any qvestions?"

"No, Mama," said Christian quietly. Fear overtook him as he thought about Mama's descriptions of fish, frogs and birds. His stomach churned as they headed back to their little mushroom house on the shelf.

As usual, Magda followed him back into his room. He flopped onto his bed and threw an arm over his face. He was not in the mood to talk.

"I'm so excited! I wish I could go with you, Christian!"

"Go away," Christian muttered.

"What?" Magda said. "Why? Are you mad at me? It's not my fault that Mama and Papa won't let me go with you."

"Magda, please...just go away and leave me alone." Christian's eyes burned. He did not want his sister to see him cry. He peeked out under his arm.

"Christian, what's the matter with you? You're going on a great big adventure tomorrow!" She added dreamily, "After that, you'll get your new shoes and a conical." She placed her hands together against her cheek and swayed from side to side.

Christian thrust his arm from his face onto his bed. "Magda, did you see all that stuff I have to worry about? Ponds, fish, frogs and birds? Plus, Papa told me to watch out for snakes and spiders and mice and skunks and squirrels and that old woodchuck that lives under the shed. He's so much bigger than me; he could swallow me in one bite!"

"Oh, Christian!" Magda giggled. "You'll be all

right. Nothing bad will happen to you! Pith will watch over you."

"Yes, but Pith cannot do anything in our realm. Wait, you know about Pith?"

Magda nodded. "Of course I do, silly. Don't you?"

Christian nodded and continued, "But, Pith members don't have bodies here, in our realm. They can't pull a bird off me, or scare a snake or pull a mouse's whiskers! All they can do is signal Papa. By the time he gets to me, I'll be filling some creature's belly!"

"Well..." Magda said. Christian could tell the ideas rattled her by the way she stilled and stared at her hands. "Didn't Papa show you what to do?"

"He gave me some pointers and told me stories, but he could not prepare me for all possibilities! I'll have to find my own food and water and fix my shelter, but if something happens near that pond, I'm no swimmer - you know that! I have my knife, but I've never had to use it for anything besides cutting food before." Christian rolled to face the wall and put his arm back over his head. "I don't want to have to hurt anyone or anything," he said in a muffled voice. "Just leave me alone. Pleeeease,

Magda."

"Ok, Christian, I'll go, but don't worry. The Master will watch over you."

Christian groaned as his door closed.

He lay in bed the rest of the evening with a stomachache, falling asleep before dinner. As he drifted off, giant wings flapped and slithery s's rang through his head.

CHAPTER 7

The next morning dawned cool and sunny. Christian got up and dressed, making sure to wear his green shirt, and then brushed his teeth.

"At least nobody will make me brush my teeth while I'm gone," he muttered, while studying himself in the mirror. He checked over his shoulder to make certain he was alone, and then he hid his toothbrush behind the water pitcher. He combed his hair and put on his beanie before going downstairs for breakfast.

"Hi ho, Tanny!" said his father with his arms outstretched, waiting for a hug. Christian leaned in, but left his arms hanging at his sides. "What's this then, son? Why the long face?"

"I'm kinda nervous, Papa..." Christian sat down

at the table.

"Of course you are, Tanny! Every smart gnome is nervous before his mission." His father chuckled. "Nerves can be a good thing – they keep you on your edge. Don't worry so - I have faith in you."

"Good morning, Christian," said his mother, "vould ya like a bean vit yer porridge taday? Ve'll get ya good and filled up before ya leave." Her hands fluttered in the air as she went to get the porridge pot.

"Sure, Mama." Christian watched his mother spoon porridge into one bowl, and then put a bean on a platter. His stomach felt better this morning, but he was not sure he could eat as much as she was putting in his bowl.

"Oh, my gnomeling," she gushed, hugging him hard as her eyes welled with tears. "I can't believe ya've grown up so already! Ya be careful out dere, Tanny. Use yer compass or knife ta send a reflection if ya get in a thorny way. Papa, Uncle Rupert or I vill be at da vindow vatching fer ya."

Christian's head perked up. "Really?"

She nodded, wiped away her tears, and gave him a quivering smile. His stomach growled. Feeling a little better, he ate with gusto.

After breakfast, Christian donned his coat and shoes, and then lifted his bag over his shoulder. When his mother asked if he had everything, he rolled his eyes and checked his bag one last time. "Compass, blanket, knife, canteen, drawing supplies...yup!"

She walked to the side table and picked up a leaf-wrapped package. "I made dese rosemary buns fer yer journey. Dere should be plenty ta see ya trough."

Christian thanked and hugged his mother.

Magda looked at him with watery eyes so he leaned in and hugged her too. He stepped lighter today. *Now that the time has come, this is pretty exciting!*

His father made sure the Andersons had left for the day and then jump-climbed down the bookshelf, leading the way ahead of Christian. They headed toward the back door in the laundry room.

"Good morn!" cried Uncle Rupert, before he fell in step behind them. Christian felt very grown up, walking with the older gnomes and he held his head higher.

His father and uncle worked together to open the back door. They pushed a step stool over to the door, and then Uncle Rupert climbed up onto its seat. He reached and heaved, struggling for a few minutes before he was finally able to twist the knob far enough around to unlatch the door. He climbed down, and then they pushed the stool back before struggling to pull the door open.

His father gave Christian a hearty hug and said, "Good luck, Son. See you soon. May your journey flow as easily as petals on the wind."

Uncle Rupert clapped him on the back and said gruffly, "You'll do great, Tanny!"

Smiling and nodding at them both, Christian took a deep breath and stepped through the door.

CHAPTER 8

The door clacked shut behind him as Christian dropped down the step to the brick path. He jumped at the sound. He glanced quickly back at the door before turning to face his surroundings. Loneliness overwhelmed him, but screwing up his courage, he took another deep breath to slow his pounding heart.

Large colored leaves fell like rain, enrapturing him. Sadness left him as he realized he had never been outside in the autumn. The air smelled crisp and chilled his hands. Stepping on a leaf, it crackled and broke apart. Christian laughed and stomped a few more times on the leaf, watching it turn into tiny pieces that the wind caught and carried away.

He could see the neighbor's house over the tall

grass in the distance and decided to check his direction. He rubbed his hand along the soft worn flap of the shoulder bag as he opened it. Mama had made the bag from an old leather human shoe and it moved easily against his body. She had sewn two pockets on the inside. One contained his tools and supplies, while the other contained her homemade buns. The green blanket lay rolled up in the bottom.

He reached inside the tool pocket and fished out the worn brass compass, accidentally pulling out and spreading daisy petals across the blanket. He gathered them together and stuck them back in the pocket before examining the compass.

He watched the magnetic needle jostle a bit before

it landed on N, for north.

Needing to go southwest, he took a long diagonal step to the left and then walked straight forward, keeping his eyes on the compass. He reached the grass in just a few minutes.

Searching the tall strands that stood above his head, he froze for a moment in panic, wondering how he would make his way through.

This grass is so much taller than it looked. I can't see anything in front of me but grass and dead leaves. I wish I had a machete to hack my way through, like in that one book I read. Now I understand why my parents said it would take three days to get there. I'm going to have to chop my way through. Good thing I brought a knife.

He took out the knife. Studying it, he hoped it would be sharp enough for the job. He held it aloft, ready to attack the foliage as he stepped into the green.

The shiny strands, damp with dew and sticky on the front sides, slid aside easier than he had expected, surprising him. The edges looked sharp, but when he reached to touch one, it did not cut him.

He took several steps into the thick grassy jungle

before it occurred to him that he had better check his direction again, so he looked at the compass a second time.

Already off course, he had veered due west. He turned one step left and resumed walking, watching the needle until he was sure of his direction.

He stuck the compass in his jacket pocket so he could access it quickly, realizing how readily the tall grass could confuse his sense of direction.

Brushing along the strands grew uncomfortable and tiring, but he squared his shoulders with fortitude and strode onward.

As time passed he became bored staring at only grass and leaves. *I wonder what Magda's doing right now.* His thoughts floated from her to his mother, which brought to mind those rosemary buns she had made. His stomach growled, but he ignored it.

Before long, he came upon a rock in a small clearing. It was just the right height for him to sit upon, so he dropped his bag to the ground, along with his canteen. Carrying his bag across his body one way and his canteen the opposite way strained his shoulders, making him glad for the break. He sat down on the rock, propped an elbow on his knee, rested his face in his hand, and looked around to investigate his surroundings.

A ladybug settled on a piece of grass, so he took his dye-stick and a clean petal from his bag, and sketched it. Drawing it caused greater interest in the insect and Christian wanted to touch the shiny surface. He stood up and reached out, but the little beetle spread its red and black shell and took flight.

Christian sighed.

When his stomach growled again, his mind drifted back to Mama's buns. The journey had gone well so far, but he still had a long way to go before nightfall. *I'd better save the buns. I think I'll give the grass a try.*

He put away the drawing supplies and reached for a nearby grass blade, tugging at the stem. It barely moved.

"Uh-oh." He stood up and pulled again. It moved slightly, but the ground would not release the stem. Christian started to panic at the thought of not being able to access food, so he anchored his feet and gave the stalk a whole-hearted wrench. Out slid the grass, and down went Christian, landing on his backside.

"Ouch!" He rubbed his bottom and slid back up

onto the rock.

"Dumb grass!" He gave the fallen blade the stink eye, and then he kicked it, looking around quickly. *I'd be so embarrassed if anyone saw me fall down.*

He stared at the grass stalk. He no longer wanted to eat from it, but after all that effort thought he'd at least better try it. He picked up the blade, turning it first one way and then the other. Light reflected off the front differently than the back. The lightness in weight surprised him, because it had taken him such strength to pull it from the ground. *Next time I'll just cut it with my knife.*

He ran his hand down the sticky front, studying the details of the piece of grass, and realized that if he cut it, he would remove the juicy part. *That's not going to work. I hope they aren't all this hard to pull out!*

Christian lifted the flat portion with his left hand, thinking how the long length resembled one of those Alpine horns he had seen in a book. Holding the tube portion in his right hand, he put his mouth on the end and sucked. Some juice dribbled down his chin, so he wiped it away with his sleeve.

"Mmm." *Not bad. I wonder if it will make a horn sound if I blow through it.*

He blew, but no sound came out. As he struggled trying again, Christian heard rustling behind him.

He stiffened. When the rustling quit, he released his head from rigid mode and looked around. When he saw nothing, he unstiffened the rest of his body. He slowly turned around for a better look. Keeping his eyes peeled to the fluttering grass, Christian dropped the blade he was holding and reached into his bag for his knife.

A dark shadow rose up amongst the foliage.

Sweat broke out on Christian's forehead and his knees shook.

When they smacked together, it roused him from his terrified state. He pulled his hand from his bag and ducked low behind the rock, to watch and wait.

The grass surged and slacked.

A large pink nose popped through.

CHAPTER 9

Under the shadow of the nose, Christian noticed his bag and canteen lying on the ground in front of the rock. Keeping his terrified eyes on the nose, he jumped up and grabbed them, running back around the rock and into the grass. The canteen jangled wildly in one hand while the shoulder bag bounced unrestrained in the other. Both banged against his body as he loped and bounced his way through the green jungle, clumsily trying to get away from whatever was attached to the big pink nose. His knees sprang up so high they almost hit his elbows. He heard rustling behind him again, so ran even harder.

Oh rose-spurs! Christian dodged this way and that. *What should I do?*

He broke through into another larger clearing, which stopped him up short. He had been running for quite some time, so he quit running on the opposite side, turned around, and bent over to catch his breath. He listened keenly as the swishing of the grass grew louder.

I can't run anymore. I must stand and face this thing. He quickly slung his bag and canteen over his shoulders, across his body. Then he dug his heels into the ground and crouched slightly. He once again was digging in his bag for his knife, when the nose popped into the clearing.

Christian froze like a human, instead of stiffening gnome-style into a statue. He stood enthralled, hand on the knife inside his bag. His heart pounded as grayish brown fur emerged behind the nose into the clearing, quickly followed by tall ears and paws bigger than his own feet. Two paws popped through the grass at the same time and hit the ground hard, causing him to jump.

Oh...it's a rabbit.

When the animal's mouth opened to show big buckteeth, Christian took a couple steps backwards.

The nose wriggled and made sniffing sounds as the whiskers poked blades of grass. One of the rabbit's eyes focused on Christian. Christian slowly eased the knife from his bag, heart racing, and held it out in front of him.

What had that book said about rabbits? Hmm, oh yeah, they're herbivores, which means they don't eat meat. Christian relaxed slightly, watching the rest of the animal enter the clearing. The bunny made no move toward him. It just sat still, watching him with one eye.

After a while, when the rabbit had made no further move toward him, Christian put the knife back in his bag and said, "Why, you're not so scary."

He nervously held out a hand toward the bunny as a show of good will.

The rabbit hopped closer and twitched its nose at Christian's hand, then moved on to sniff his coat and legs. When the bunny bonked Christian's face with its nose, Christian laughed. He a moment before gently touching the bunny's cheek and rubbing the fur down its face.

"Why, you're just a baby, aren't you?" Christian said.

The bunny stilled. *It must like me petting it.*

Christian rubbed the soft fur toward the top of the bunny's head and scratched between its ears.

While Christian petted, the bunny gently lowered itself down into the grass, laid its head on its paws, and closed its eyes.

"Your nose doesn't seem all that big now that I get a closer look at it." Christian said, chuckling as he studied the damp pink feature.

Christian rubbed the bunny's fur for a few minutes and then he paused, lifting his hand gently away from the fur. The bunny slept, so he pulled the compass back out to check his direction. He headed into the grass, looking backward once more at the fuzzy creature and shook his head, remembering his intense fear.

***

Christian walked a few more hours, only slowing to snack on a grass blade now and then or to avoid cobwebs and slippery mucky leaves. He barely noticed his surroundings, practicing the message over and over in his head. Eventually he reached the side of the Andersons' car pad and stopped to take in his current surroundings. *This ledge is really high, but at least I can still see the Beezleys' house over it. I'll follow it around. It'll be an easy guide to where I'll set up camp for the night.*

Hunger pangs brought him from his

contemplation, so he hoisted himself up onto the ledge and dug one of his mother's rosemary buns from his bag. Drinking water on and off all day caused his canteen to be nearly empty. He took one small sip and left the rest for camp. The bun stuck in his throat, making him thirstier, but his belly felt better. The bun also warmed his heart. *Just a little bit of home - thanks, Mama.*

Finishing the bun, he brushed away the crumbs, dropped down from the ledge, and resumed his hike. Christian bounced a hand up and down along the wall while he walked, both to guide himself and as a distraction from his thirst. He stopped at the site of an unusual tree and took a few minutes to draw it.

After a little while, the light began to fade, so he tucked the drawing in his bag with the other used petal.

His adrenaline, which had spiked from the bunny incident, wore off and his legs began to ache. Tired and bored, he began to hum. Before long, he heard another rustling behind him.

This time instead of running, he turned around slowly. He hunched his shoulders and braced his feet, but he did not have the breath or strength to run again. Weary, wary and apprehensive, but not as frightened as the first time he'd heard the close noises, he waited with one hand in his bag, on the knife.

The bunny poked its nose out of the grass again. Christian let go of the knife, shook his head, and then gestured to the creature. "Oh, alright then, come on."

He resumed walking, humming, and bouncing his hand along the ledge until they turned the corner. The bunny kept pace with him, taking small hops and occasionally bumping into Christian. Exhausted, Christian barely noticed when the bunny's nose bumped his back.

This side of the car pad was harder to traverse. Christian carefully made his way over gravel, weeds, and around the occasional dead bug.

When he finally came to the end of the pavement, Christian dropped his canteen and bag to the ground and plopped down. He leaned against the side of the car pad to rest for a few minutes. The bunny hunched down quietly next to him, twitching its nose and whiskers. A whisker caught Christian under the chin and tickled him. He giggled and rubbed the bunny's face, but when he stopped petting, the bunny nudged Christian for more. Christian petted him for a while until eventually he pulled himself away to set up camp.

The bunny watched Christian tramp down a wide oval in the grass to make a flat place to sleep. When he finished that job, Christian pulled his blanket from the bag and sat down again, to finish his water. He shivered from the cold, so he rubbed the soft blanket against his face, thinking of his bed in his warm room at home.

The bunny hunkered down next to Christian, and as he stroked its fur, Christian thought back over his first day in the outdoors. *I have been hungry, thirsty, tired and scared, but I'm glad to have this quiet friend. Now I don't have to spend the night alone.*

Christian fell asleep on the bunny.

CHAPTER 10

"I'm hungry."

"What?" Christian muttered groggily, struggling to wake up.

"I'm hungry."

Christian rubbed his eyes and looked around sleepily. All of a sudden he jumped up, clutching his blanket. *Who said that?*

Nobody was there with him, except for the bunny.

Weird. I must've been dreaming. He shook his head and began to roll up his blanket.

"I'm hungry."

Christian dropped the blanket and quickly stepped back. He stared at the bunny.

"Is that you?" he asked, scratching his head. "Are

you speaking to me?"

"Yes, it's me. I'm hungry." The bunny slowly blinked at Christian. Christian shook his head as he looked into the bunny's black eyes. *What is happening here?*

He leaned down to retrieve his blanket and noticed the grass below the bunny's face had been chomped down to dirt.

The bunny sat hunched very still and blinking, continuing to stare at Christian.

"I'm hungry," it said again. Christian tossed the blanket onto his bag.

Bewildered, Christian shook his head, nodding at the bunny. He looked around for a moment, and then reached toward a piece of taller grass. The blade slid out easier than the day before, covered in damp morning dew. He fed it to the bunny, which chewed the blade slowly and thoroughly, showing flashes of its long white teeth. When the bunny finished, it slowly blinked at Christian again.

When Christian continued to stare back at the bunny, it repeated, "I'm hungry."

Christian repeated the process eight more times until the bunny closed its eyes and lowered its head back down onto its paws.

Christian wiped his wet hands on his pants. He took a bun from his bag for his own breakfast. The bunny opened his eyes and sniffed, inching its nose closer to the rosemary bun. Christian took a bite.

"Mmm..."

He broke off a piece and handed it to the bunny. After it finished eating its chunk, the bunny rubbed its nose up and down Christian's arm while he finished his portion. Whiskers tickled him again as Christian thought, *I'm still hungry.*

He stood up, picked a few grass stems and drank the sweet nectar. The bunny watched him, but said nothing more.

"I'm glad Papa told me about the grass. It helps both the hunger and the thirst." He spoke to the bunny, unaware if it understood him or not. *I miss Papa...and Mama...and even Magda.*

He imagined them at breakfast and wondered if they were having beans with their porridge today. Then he shook his head. *I want to go home.*

Christian bent to pick up his blanket, but saw the empty canteen lying on the ground, and looked swiftly to the grass. He picked the canteen up instead of the blanket, and walked over to the tall stalks.

Oooo, I'd better hurry or I won't have any water to drink today. The grass is almost dry already.

He pulled at the tip of a grass blade, bending it into an arc toward him. Beads of dew collected and slid down the stalk, where he funneled them into his canteen. Only a few drops were needed to fill the canteen to bursting. Slightly dehydrated and thirsty, he drank deeply and then collected more.

Christian rolled up his blanket, now damp with bits of leaves and grass, and put it inside his bag. Then he took off his jacket to shake off the vegetation that clung to it. When it was as clean as shaking could make it, he put it back on. Then he slung his bag over one shoulder and the canteen back over the other one. Looking around, certain he had gathered all of his belongings; he faced the bunny with his hands on his hips.

"Well, are you ready to go?" he asked.

The bunny blinked at him, but said nothing. He glanced once more around the campsite and said, "I'm leaving now, if you want to come along."

The bunny lifted its head, looked at Christian, blinked, and laid its head back down.

"Okay, then, see ya!" Christian checked his

compass and walked into the grass, waving at the bunny.

CHAPTER 11

Christian grew frustrated at the grass. Parts of it had not yet been exposed to the sun and were still wet. Blades slapped against him as he walked, soaking his pants and boots. Even though the grass did not seem hard to part and push through, his arms soon began to ache. Luckily, as it dried, the hike became easier and Christian's mood lightened.

I feel pretty good. I slept well, nestled in with that warm, furry bunny.

Now that he was back out on his own and a little more confident after a full day's experience, Christian began to pay more attention to his surroundings.

He picked up drying leaf bits, studying the different types as he hiked. He saw several types of grasses, and delightedly identified thistles, clovers, and dandelions from Mama's recipes.

As he was walking and looking to the side, he bumped straight into a skull. He immediately stiffened into rigid mode and his heart pounded. *Death. Right here in the grass.*

He stood still a long while, unsure of what to do, but soon realized he could not stay in that place indefinitely. There was no movement around him so he eventually screwed up his courage, unstiffened and turned to look hard at the skull. *Aww, thistle-stickers! It's just one of those withering snapdragons from Mama's book – not a creature's skull at all. Do I feel dumb! Such a waste of time, standing there so long.*

Christian looked at the flower again and found it intriguing. He decided to pull out his dye-stick and a new petal to quickly draw it.

Soon he resumed his hike, drawing and analyzing flora with a new intensity. He kept it up for a couple of hours, until he came upon a roundish pile of muck.

"Oh, what in the herb garden is that?" he howled, pinching his nose against the smell. He checked his boots to make sure he had not stepped in the nasty gunk, and noticed a foot bone sticking out of it. *If I shrink this, I bet it won't stink so badly.*

He put his hands together and brought them to his face, but before he could work his magic, something in the pile caught his eye. He peered closer. *A feather. Hmm...the feather's cool... Wonder if I could use it. Seems a shame to just leave it here. Maybe I could put dye in it for drawing.*

Just then, the grass rustled. Christian jerked, startled as the sound pulled him from his concentration. He turned.

"Hello, bunny."

His new friend hopped closer, but when it saw the pile, it growled.

"Why are you growling?"

Christian looked back at the pile. *Bones.*

"Owl."

Christian heard the word and looked from the pile back to the bunny. *I must be losing my mind if that bunny can talk. Wait a minute... Owls eat small prey.*

He stepped backwards from the pile and looked up. His eyes scanned the sky franticly as the bunny continued growling. Its eyes also turned skyward.

This stinks! There is danger everywhere! Maybe I should just turn around and go home.

After a few moments passed with no sighting of the great beast that had vomited the stinky pile, Christian decided it was time to go, just in case the bird came back. He picked up the feather, wiped it on the grass, stuck it in his cap, and trudged back into the green. The bunny was fast on his heels this time, all signs of sleepiness gone.

Fear spiked his adrenaline so Christian moved quickly, and the bunny kept pace for a while. They eventually tired and slowed; but continued to push forward, putting as much distance as possible between them and the pile.

Christian led the way, slogging clumsily through the grass. As they came upon a dead spot, they stumbled upon a brown spider with a swiggly shape on its back.

Christian stopped in his tracks and threw out a hand so the bunny could not pass him. His pulse picked up speed and he held his breath, watching the spider weave a web between two branches of a stick. The spider did not notice them, at first. *What did that book say about spiders? The indoor ones aren't harmful as long as I stay out of their way, so maybe the outdoor spiders aren't either?*

Christian took a quick step backwards, tripping on a stone and bumping into the bunny. He grasped at the bunny's fur, righting himself. He kept ahold of the fur with one hand as he heaved himself back up. Christian felt the bunny's head sway from him to the spider and then back, but he stood still and kept his eyes on the spider.

The bunny lifted a paw, which rustled the grass. The spider slowly turned to face them, pausing only a moment before it began crawling toward them.

Christian's knees wobbled.

He pulled the knife from his bag and held it out, just as he had when practicing with his sword needle. The spider grew bigger the closer it came. Sweat popped out on Christian's forehead. The creature stood as tall as his knees.

"Stop right there!" he hollered.

That spider ignored him and kept coming. A bead of sweat ran down the side of Christian's face. He slashed at the spider. The spider leaned back, and then ran at him. Stepping backwards, Christian stumbled and fell to the ground.

Fear paralyzed him. He forgot to stiffen.

"No." The bunny stood on its hind legs.

The bunny's a giant when it stands on two legs!

Both front paws pounced down on the spider, squashing it dead.

Christian stared at the squashed spider for a long time, waiting for his heart rate to slow; and then he looked at the bunny.

"D-d-did you speak to me again?"

The bunny stared back at Christian, wriggling its nose and whiskers.

Christian covered his ears and shook his head from side to side. He abruptly sat up cross-legged in the grass.

"What is happening to me?" he asked, feeling dazed.

Christian tried to hold his shaking hands still and took a few deep breaths. The bunny squatted down beside him. Overwhelmed, Christian reached for the soft fur.

Rubbing the bunny's back finally stilled the shaking of his hands.

Christian removed his canteen and took a swig.

The bunny stretched and lay down.

Christian resumed petting it, and grew sleepy. He laid his head upon the soft downy fur and closed his eyes. *I'm just going to rest a moment.*

He promptly fell asleep.

When he awoke much later, he sat up groggily. The sun had traveled low on the horizon, so he jumped up. Adjusting his cap, he stepped carefully around the dead spider and past the web on the twigs, heading straight into the grass. He checked his compass as he walked. He needed to make it to the rocks Mama had told him about before dark.

When he realized the bunny was not following him, he turned around and went back. He shook the bunny awake, beckoned with a wave and once the bunny was standing, marched back into the grass.

Relief flooded through him when he heard the grass rustle behind him.

It was not long before the bunny nudged his back. Christian stopped and looked at the bunny in the lowering light.

"I suppose you're hungry, huh, girl?" Christian bent his head and lifted his bag flap.

"Boy."

Christian's hand stilled and he turned back to the bunny. "What?"

Nothing.

Christian thought for a moment and asked, "Did you say you are a boy?"

No answer came, but the bunny's nose twitched back and forth. Christian resumed walking and dug in his bag, taking out another of his mother's delicious buns.

"Here."

He tore off half and pushed it into the bunny's mouth. The bunny chewed the herby treat quickly. When Christian saw how fast the bunny ate its portion, he shoved his piece all the way into his own mouth. He did not want to have to share any more of his bun. If he was going to have to share with the bunny, he needed to ration them carefully, to make sure there were enough for the entire journey.

Mama had always told him to be prepared, because you never knew what or who was around the next corner. *Ah, Mama. Gnomes never know when the unexpected or delays may happen.*

Christian sighed.

He took a drink from his canteen, and then poured a bit into the bunny's mouth.

Christian considered his predicament. The nap set him back and he tried to estimate how much more time it would take to get to the rocks. He had not been able to see them through the grass that morning when he began his hike, but last night as he had looked across the yard from the corner of the car pad, he thought he knew about where they lay. He scrunched his face up; trying to remember if there was a spot anywhere in between that he could camp, but none came to mind.

To stave off the fear that was creeping in on him, he began to hum a song his Mama had sung to him and Magda when they were much younger. *It's just me and the bunny after all – there's nobody else around to care.*

Christian's humming turned to singing:

"Papa carved me a game, called gnomie come home...

then a friend of mine came, I couldn't play it alone.

I threw the sandbag... and it hit the high mark...

I moved my gnome forward... and my friend's mood went dark.

He magic'd the sandbag... it grew and grew...

He cheated the game, until the sandbag blew."

His voice grew louder as his fear subsided.

> "Sand covered the target, numbers seen no more...
>
> I shouted at him... you'd better clean up this floor.
>
> His anger swiftly dropped, as his eyes grew wide...
>
> he swept up the sand... we both sat down and sighed.
>
> A game is no fun, when one gnomie gets mad,
>
> it will ruin a friendship...and that is sad, sad, sad."

"Hee he hee he, hee he hee he."

Christian whipped around to look at the bunny.

"That's funny."

"Bunny?"

"Yes..."

"Are you speaking to me?"

"Why, of course, silly! I've been speaking to you the whole time. Sometimes you can hear..."

Nothing.

"ERRRRG!" grumbled Christian, turning and stomping onward.

His anger increased his momentum. The bunny's hops grew longer to keep up with Christian's faster pace, which caused more disruption and noise in the grass. They were making too loud of a commotion. *Someone or something is going to hear us – maybe even an owl or a hawk.*

Christian shivered and slowed, dropping back to walk in line with the bunny. *Maybe I shouldn't sing so loudly either.*

CHAPTER 12

"Hey, thanks for getting that spider for me."

They had stopped to rest and now Christian stood up, struggling as his bag and canteen clanked around him.

The bunny's nose twitched. Christian quelled his rising frustration. *That bunny is trying to talk to me right now – I just know it!*

Christian bent low to check if the bunny's mouth was moving under its big nose, but as he lowered his head, the bunny's head followed so he could not tell. He shook his head and took a swig from his canteen. Then he held the canteen up, offering water to the bunny. It lifted its head and dropped its mouth open, so Christian tipped a few drops into it.

When they resumed walking, Christian's mood cheered. *I can hear the bunny talk... Sometimes at least!*

Buoyed by his new awareness, he belted out another song.

"Alas, my love, you do me wrong,

to cast me off discourteously...

for I have loved you well and long,

delighting in your company!"

And then louder still,

"Greensleeves was all my joy,

Greensleeves was my delight,

Greensleeves was my heart of gold,

and who but my lady Greensleeves."

As Christian sang, the bunny hopped ahead, and then dropped onto its back in another small clearing of dead grass. It clutched at its belly with its front paws and kicked its back legs repeatedly, rolling back and forth. Christian laughed and sat down beside the bunny on the ground.

"I'm glad you think my singing is so funny," Christian said, after his laughing had subsided. "But I wish I could hear you speak now."

The bunny finally quieted and nudged Christian's hand with its nose. Christian rubbed the nose and then stood up.

"Well, we'd better get going." He brushed the grass off his pants and then patted the bunny's head again. "I'm glad you're with me."

The bunny hopped after Christian across the clearing.

"I think it's this way," he said, looking at his compass, straining to read the letters. The light was almost gone as they headed back into the foliage.

A few minutes later Christian paused and said, "I just don't know if we should stop or keep going. I would really like to reach those rocks Mama told me about, if we can," he looked at the sky, "before dark."

The bunny trembled and looked up.

"I was thinking that those large birds are going to be out anytime now," the bunny said.

Christian paused and stared at the bunny. *Wow*.

Then he realized what the bunny had said. He searched the sky, patting its side.

They resumed their hike. The light grew dim.

Rocks bloomed before them. Christian stopped in his tracks, and stared at them.

"Oh! I'm so glad we made it!" Breathing a sigh of relief, he plopped down and dropped his stuff beside him.

Leaning back against a rock, he fished another bun from his bag and shared it. Then he swallowed the last of his water and picked out a few grass blades to round out their supper.

Christian searched the rocks and easily found the chipped spot his mother had told him about. He gathered dead grass clippings and packed them into the crevice underneath. It would be tight, but he could just squeeze his body into the space. When he pulled out his blanket and lay down, the bunny snuggled up close to him.

Christian was completely hidden, but noticed that the bunny was only partially disguised from a predator's view. Since the dead grass and the bunny's fur provided warmth for Christian, he crawled out and covered the bunny with his blanket, for added protection. The bunny remained calm enough to fall asleep through Christian's fumbling, and then Christian crawled back into the crevice to lie down. He stared out past the bunny's ears at the stars. *I should get there tomorrow night – right on time.*

Before long, the sound of the crickets lulled him to sleep.

***

Morning broke in a damp foggy haze. Christian stretched and nudged the bunny. It did not move. He nudged the bunny again. Nothing. He crawled out of the space and removed the blanket. The cool air finally penetrated the deep sleep of the bunny and it began to wriggle its nose.

"Good morning, bunny!" said Christian, rolling up the blanket. He packed it into his bag.

"Sleep."

"Well, I have to get back on my journey." Christian put his hands on his hips. "You can stay and sleep if you want, but I'm going." Christian waited.

The bunny lifted an eyelid, and then dropped it again. "Sleep."

Christian sucked on some grass ends and refilled his canteen. He meandered around the campsite, pulling extra blades of grass for the bunny. He laid them next to its nose.

"Well, here I go…" Christian said, hopeful that the bunny would finally get up and come with him. When the bunny continued to sleep, Christian looked at his compass, glanced once more at the bunny and shook his head, then slowly walked back into the green.

After walking for a couple of hours, Christian took a break to sit upon a rock and sketch. He tried to draw the bunny, but the heavy fog caused the daisy petal to hang limply, so he was unable to make good solid lines. Frustrated, he threw the petal to the ground, but it stuck to his pants on the way down. Every piece of his clothing was wet from the damp morning grass that slapped at his legs.

He grew cold as he sat. He ate a bun, glad to have the whole thing to himself, and drank some water. *I'll warm up again if I keep walking.*

His muscles ached. *Trudging through this wet grass, hiking more than I've ever done in my whole gnome life, and sleeping outside...it's no wonder I'm tired. Maybe I should have stayed back with the bunny and slept a little longer. He had the right idea. I should have followed his example.*

As he hiked, Christian's eyes closed halfway in a trance-like state. He wandered over the edge of a hill, lost his footing, and tumbled. He slipped and slid down the hill of wet leaves and grass - straight into the pond.

"Op, oop, kk, uff," he sputtered, splashing his arms around. Struggling to regain his balance,

Christian could not stay upward long enough to grip the bottom with his feet.

Something yanked at his shoe. Christian flailed about wildly. His head ducked under the water.

Something brushed past his hand. He couldn't catch his breath so he grabbed at it, but missed. Christian's eyes were clenched tightly closed and he was beginning to see spots on the back of his eyelids.

The thing brushed by again.

This time he grasped it, clutching tightly to anything to right himself, as the bunny pulled him up from the water - just in time to avoid the coy fish that jumped at him, mouth wide open. *That is one gaping black hole I could slide right into!*

Both the bunny and Christian fell back upon the grass. They lay there for quite some time catching their breath and letting water drip from fur and clothing.

"Narrrow essscape," croaked a deep voice from above.

Christian sat up and looked around, but saw no one.

"You arrre a lucky one," the voice gargled.

Christian turned to look behind himself. A large

fat frog with a white belly and spotted green back sat hunched on a rock nearby, flicking the air with its long tongue. Its black eyes blinked slowly at him, watching.

He jerked to his feet. The bunny also lifted itself up onto its front paws, to stand beside Christian. The bunny stared blankly at the frog.

"What'sss with the rrrabbit?" croaked the frog. "Why'd he sssave you in the waterrr?" He hopped off the rock.

"He's m-my friend," answered Christian with a slight stutter, shivering from a mix of cold and fear at the frog's huge size. He leaned into the bunny. "He's saved me m-more than once on my mission.

Hey, where'd you come from anyway?" Christian rubbed the bunny's leg for reassurance, his mind briefly flashing on the spider and remembering the cold of night.

"I've neverrr sssseen a rrrabbit do anything like that beforrre." The frog blinked and hopped closer. "What's a misssion?"

"It's a job I have to do so I can earn my conical hat and mystical shoes. Where did you say you came from? Is this your pond?" asked Christian, looking around and stepping back.

"I live herrre..." the frog croaked, not adding any extra helpful information, but flicking its tongue in the air and hopping closer.

Christian caught himself wringing his hands. *That thing is huge. I must not show fear.*

He dropped them and stood taller.

"Well, I think we'll be going."

The frog hopped closer. Christian took another step backwards, moving his hand from the bunny's leg to its back.

"Well...now wait jussst a moment," croaked the frog, opening its mouth wide near Christian.

"Hey! What are you doing?" yelled Christian, swiping at his pants.

"Jussst getting a sssssniff…"

"Well, you don't need to sniff me!"

The frog's sticky tongue struck out and caught Christian's arm. Christian lost his footing and clutched at the bunny. The frog wrestled him just a moment, and then let him go.

"Ewwww! Knock it off, frog!" Christian swiped the mucus off his arm with his other hand. He tried to shake the mucus onto the ground, but it clung to his hand.

"Niccce," croaked the frog. "What are you? You taste like grrrasss and sssomething elssse…"

"Rosemary," said Christian automatically, thinking of Mama's buns. "Hey, wait. Stop trying to smell and taste me!" he yelled and stomped, slapping at the tongue that came at him again. The frog did not get ahold of Christian that time. He looked around for something to throw at the frog.

"Calm down, calm down…" said the frog, flicking his tongue again. "Outhhhh!"

Christian's eyebrows shot up in surprise when he looked down. The bunny's paws sat on the frog's tongue and he was leaning into it, weighing the tongue down.

"Okay, Okay…" he sputtered, trying to talk

around the bunny's paws without using his tongue. "I'llll quiiit!"

Christian thought about it for a moment and then nodded to the bunny. The bunny released the frog's tongue.

"Hey, what's your deal, anyway? Frogs don't eat gnomes, they eat flies," Christian said angrily, smearing mucus from his hands onto a grass blade. "Look what you've done to my pants!"

Sucking noises filled the air as he pulled his wet and slime-covered pants away from his legs.

The bunny's nose twitched and it snickered, watching Christian fling more frog goo onto the grass. Christian scowled at it and pointed to its paws. The bunny stopped snickering and twitching when it saw the goo covering them. It had as little luck as Christian when it tried to wipe its paws on the ground.

Both Christian and the bunny turned back toward the frog to complain, but it was already mid-jump into the water.

"Well, that woke me up a bit! Wait a minute... I could hear every word he said. Are you talking to me now?"

The bunny nodded. "I..."

That was all Christian heard.

"Oh, weeds and twigs! Let's go," he said, gesturing at the bunny to follow him. He plodded away from the pond, listening to his boots squelch. He was wet and cold and wanted to get away from the frog as soon as gnomely possible.

CHAPTER 13

Christian slogged along, collecting bits of grass and leaves on his sticky pants. The bunny hopped beside him. As time went by, the bunny's fur dried and dropped the bits and pieces it had picked up. By the time they finally made it up the hill to the side of the neighbor's house, the bunny appeared almost as clean as normal. *I wish the bits had dropped off of my pants!*

Christian took a drink from his canteen, gave one to the bunny and then patted its shoulder.

"Well, here're the bushes Mama showed me. The window should be just under there." Christian pointed to a dark spot. "You can't go with me in there, boy, but I'm going to return home, so if you want to wait for me, well... I wouldn't mind. I'll understand if you have to go, though. If you go, I wish you good travels," Christian said, with a sniff. *Saying good-bye is hard. I hope he waits.*

The bunny twitched its nose, turned around and hopped back down the hill - without a word.

Christian's shoulders drooped as he watched the bunny hop away. *I'm going to miss that bunny. I guess I'm on my own... Again.*

Loneliness suddenly overwhelmed him. His pulse raced and his stomach grew butterflies at the thought. He rubbed his churning belly as he cautiously entered a gap in the dark bushes. Once underneath them, a shaft of sunlight reflected off the window. *Whew! Not so scary.*

Tap, tap, tap.

Christian waited. When he received no response, he tapped again. Again, he received no reply. He walked out of the bushes and looked around, but saw no one. His stomach lurched again so he sat down to contemplate his next move.

Sitting on the hill, Christian could see the whole neighborhood: the road, the mailboxes, and the other houses on large plots of land. When he spotted the Andersons' house, a deep longing for home washed over him. He took out his dye-stick and a fresh petal to draw a picture of the neighborhood.

When he finished the drawing, he added it to the stack of petals in his bag. He decided to try to knock once more, and went back into the dark. He tapped. *What am I going to do if nobody answers? Maybe I should -*

"Hold onto your cap, I'm coming!" A voice bellowed from behind him. Christian left the bushes and saw a young she-gnome clutching her skirt as she climbed the hill toward him.

His eyes went wide and his mouth dropped open. Christian had led a sheltered life, and the only other young gnome he had ever seen was his sister.

Her hair is the color of those sand dollars the Andersons brought back from Hawaii.

He sighed.

As she came closer, his hand seemed to reach out to touch her hair all by itself. Luckily, he quickly gained control, dropped his hand and snapped his mouth closed when she looked up at him. *Her eyes are the color of the sea in their vacation photos.*

"What do you want?" she groaned, breathing heavily as her skirt swished back and forth across her legs. She bent over and put her hands on her knees. "Give me a minute to catch my breath. I had to run all the way from the dining room to get here. I made pretty good time, too."

After a few seconds, when she had mostly caught her breath, she stood up, placed her hands on her hips, raised an eyebrow and tapped her foot. She panted, "Well?"

Christian stared at her. He opened his mouth to speak, but no words came out.

"Cat got your tongue?" She hooted with laughter at her own joke, and then bent over to slap her leg. "If the cat's caught your tongue, he'd have more than just that! You'd be lucky if your cap was left behind."

The leg slap broke Christian's trance. He furrowed his brow and sputtered, "You're lucky a cat hasn't caught you yet!" Then Christian looked around furtively. "Is there a cat close?"

"Silly gnomie... don't you know we have several feral cats wandering this neighborhood?"

The blood drained from Christian's face.

"No, I didn't know." As he looked around again for cats, the memory of an overheard conversation between his parents slammed into his mind. He lost his breath. *How could I have forgotten about the cats!*

She looked around again, and then shrugged.

Her eyes sparkle.

"Anyway, what do you want?" she asked, resuming her foot-tapping. She folded her arms across her chest.

Her question helped Christian catch his breath. "I came from next door - the Anderson house - to deliver a message." He threw a finger up, pointing to the house.

Her gaze followed his hand and then she turned back. "Okay. What's the message?" she asked. She continued tapping and raised an eyebrow in question.

"Um...I'm to deliver it to Mrs. Beezley, herself. You don't look like a Mrs. Beezley. In fact, you don't look like much of anything," Christian said, stung as he remembered her laughing at him. *Why did I say that? That was mean. I'm not mean. Aww, rose-spurs, she's going to cry.*

The she-gnome's face scrunched up. She stared at him through squinty eyes and her lip quivered. A tear slipped down her cheek; but she swiped at it angrily.

"Aw, thistle-stickers! I'm sorry, but you made me mad when you laughed at me." His face heated as he spoke, but he patted her shoulder awkwardly.

She looked away and sniffed. "I'm sorry too. Sometimes I stick my boot in it. I was kinda mad my mother sent me out here. I don't really like coming outside by myself."

"Well, you're not by yourself anymore. I'm here. Maybe you could bring me to her?" Christian first stood taller, and then slumped again as cats flashed across his mind. He looked around.

From his vantage point on the hill, he could see more than he had ever seen from home, but luckily no cats. He turned back to the she-gnome and nodded.

He said, "Let's go inside, then we can rest a bit."

"Come on," she replied, waving her hand in a friendlier manner. "The humans are home. I have to take you up the rose trellis to Ashley's room. You're lucky she left her window open a tad; otherwise we'd have to find another way to sneak you in. Mama's waiting for us, though. She has a moth that sleeps in the curtain right above that window you tapped on and it was not happy to wake up during the day. We don't get many visitors that disturb him."

Christian shook his head. "We don't either. Why is her window open? It's kind of cold."

"She likes fresh air. She gets in trouble from her parents sometimes, though." Winny chuckled.

Christian followed the she-gnome around to the backside of the house. When they reached the trellis, Christian shifted his bag and canteen to his back. The she-gnome climbed up first.

Christian kept watch for cats as he climbed, but noticed a colorful outdoor structure that looked a bit like a house with extra wooden beams.

"Who lives there?" he asked.

"Where?"

"Right there," he said, pointing at the structure.

She laughed. "Nobody lives in it, silly! It's for the humans to play on. They get exercise there. It's a good thing too, because they sit around inside all the time. I love my Ashley, but she should go outside more. She doesn't play on it now that she's older, but she could still use the exercise, and since she likes fresh air so much..."

Christian frowned as he stared at the structure. "But that seems such a waste of space. A whole family of gnomes could live in there, with room to grow herbs and greens."

"Yeah, I know. When my Uncle Harry comes to visit, he wants to sleep out there because he normally lives outside, but Mama won't let him because of the cats. I think he could easily escape if one found him, but Mama worries."

"Really? My mother does too - too much," replied Christian sharply. He immediately regretted his words when Mama's face floated into his mind.

The she-gnome laughed. "She probably has to. I've heard that boys can get into trouble pretty easily."

Christian scowled. "I don't. And they gave me the job to bring this message, didn't they?"

"I'll bet she is worrying a lot about you, anyway."

Christian looked away. "I guess... This is my mission to earn my conical and mystical shoes."

"Oh, right. Yeah, I went through that last spring. Mine's purple," she said, feeling around on her head. "Oh, I guess I forgot to put it on before I raced outside!"

"I've never seen a purple one before."

"Purple means 'of the mind,' and my third gift is wisdom, which includes knowing the history of our people. I'm a sage, but I haven't felt much like one since I got my conical. Of course, what's there to be all sagey about anyway?" She threw out one hand in irritation, while holding onto the trellis with the other. Her face grew serious. "You should make sure to listen to me if I tell you stuff," she said. "I mean... it *is* my power after all."

"Whatever..." Christian shook his head and climbed up the last part of the trellis, close on her heels.

CHAPTER 14

When they reached the bedroom window, the gnome girl slipped over the ledge and into the room easily, but Christian caught one of his boots on a jutting nail and got stuck. He dangled against the inside wall, hanging from the window frame.

"Hey, help me!" He waved his loose leg and arms around trying to prevent his bag and canteen from falling off. His beanie fell to the floor.

The she-gnome giggled and then pulled on his arms, shaking him from side to side. His shoe came loose, and then both gnomes plopped down onto the floor as Christian's shoe flew away.

"Uffda!" said Christian. He scrambled to stand, and then smoothed his clothes and folded his arms across his chest, trying to look cool rather than clumsy. It was hard to look cool with only one shoe.

"Hey, what's your name anyway?" he asked. *Her eyes really sparkle when she laughs.*

"Winola," she said. She stood up and smoothed out her clothes before clasping her hands together in front of her apron. She shuffled her feet from side to side. "What's yours?"

"Christian." One side of his mouth lifted in a half smile as he tried out her name, "Winola... That's a mouth full."

She scowled at him, fisted her hands and stamped a foot. "I know that, duh! My friends call me Winny."

Oooo, she's gets mad easy!

Winny headed for the bedroom door. "Let's get Mama."

Christian grabbed his beanie and shoe and followed her, hopping on one foot as he put the shoe on. Not sure what had made her angry, he shook his head and replayed the conversation in his head. *Girls!*

That thought immediately brought Magda to mind. He imagined her lying on his floor talking to him. He chuckled quietly when he remembered her, as she threw his cap at him. His head drooped as a wave of sadness washed over him. Thinking of Magda led to another memory of his parents. *I am ready to finish this job and get home!*

Luckily, the bedroom door was slightly ajar when they reached it. Winny peeked into the hallway, looking first one direction, and then the other. Nodding the all clear to Christian, she pushed the door wide enough for them to fit through. They snuck across the hall floor, toward the top of the staircase.

Christian paused when she raised a hand. She edged along the last few paces to the top banister alone, and then she peered through the banister to make sure nobody was downstairs. She motioned the all clear to Christian and he followed her.

She climbed up a wooden banister leg and hopped onto the staircase railing. Then, she sat down backwards, leaned forward on her belly, and slid all the way down. Her shoes made a low squeaking sound as they trailed along the wood, and Christian quickly searched for anyone who may have heard the noise.

At the bottom, she jumped onto the landing before turning back to look up at Christian. She put one finger over her lips in a keep quiet gesture, looked around, and then waved him down.

Christian looked through the banister to the landing floor, then back at the railing, then down at the hallway floor, and shook his head at Winny. *I am not sliding down that thing!*

She scowled at him and waved again. He shook his head again, and then she scowled, nodded and stamped a foot on the carpet, waving in a hurried manner.

Christian heard noises coming from somewhere below.

Winny waved wildly at him again. Then she pushed her elbows against her waist, allowing her hands to hang limply bent at the wrist, and lolled her tongue out, while she hopped from one foot to the other. Christian shook his head and shrugged his shoulders. He looked around frantically, but could see no cause of the noise. *What is she doing? What does she mean?*

She seemed adamant and he could tell she was getting angry, so he took a couple of deep breaths, and climbed the same wooden leg. *I will not look down. I will not look down.*

He closed his eyes and slid, zinging right off the end and banging into the opposite wall on the landing. He scampered to his feet, rubbed his back, and then both gnomes quickly jump-climbed down the last three steps into the front hallway.

Clickity, clackety, clickety, clackety. Nails clicked on the tile floor. Christian jumped behind Winny as an enormous cream and tan curly-haired dog sauntered into the hallway with its tongue hanging out. It ambled over to Winny and licked her from foot to head. She laughed quietly and patted the dog.

"Hello, Biscuit," she said.

Christian watched their interaction, and then glowered at Winny.

She bashfully turned to look at him, rocking back and forth as she shifted her feet from heels to toes.

"You did not tell me there was a dog, or that it was your friend," accused Christian.

"You should have seen your face when you were upstairs!" Winny laughed as she rubbed the dog's legs. "Come on, Biscuit won't hurt you. Just let him sniff you before we go."

She grabbed Christian's hand and held it up to Biscuit's nose.

Christian flinched. His face got hot and his

stomach fluttered. He looked at their clasped hands and wanted to take that step toward the dog, but his feet planted themselves firmly to the floor. *I certainly do not want to be licked by that giant peppy creature!*

Winny studied Christian curiously, and then looked down. She dropped his hand like a hot piece of toast as her face turned red. Looking back at her cocker spaniel, she said again, "Just let him sniff you."

Christian again did not heed Winny's advice as he stared at the hairy beast. *I'm not going near that great huge thing!*

Winny waited for a moment, and then pointed at Christian. "Sniff, Biscuit!"

Christian's mouth dropped open. He cringed when the dog's giant head came down to inhale his scent. The wet nose rubbed Christian's beanie and hair as it sniffed, then moved down to his jacket. Biscuit sniffed Christian's bag, and then licked it.

"Oh, he must smell my mother's buns," Christian said, as the dog jostled him.

"Uh-oh," said Winny, pulling at the dog's fur. "Come, Biscuit!"

The dog ignored her, and continued to lick the

bag.

"No!" shouted Christian, frustrated and overwhelmed by the dog's energy. He bonked the dog's nose. Biscuit stopped licking, dropped his head and looked at Christian with the largest and saddest brown eyes he had ever seen. *I shouldn't have yelled at the poor dog.*

He petted the dog, but instantly regretted it because Biscuit licked him again.

"It's okay..." he said, pushing the dog's mouth away. Biscuit sniffed at Christian's pants, which were almost dry now from the pond incident.

Biscuit's tongue lolled from his mouth and he cocked an ear. Winny stilled. Christian heard steps.

"We have to hide, come on!" Winny hissed.

Winny ran into the living room and hid behind a crooked chair. Christian followed right behind her. Breathless, Christian turned and peeked around the chair leg just in time to see a human girl. She wore those same large black things that Zach always wore on his head, which covered their ears. She snapped her fingers while she strutted and sashayed her way up the steps, holding one of those boxy gadgets.

"That's my girl, Ashley," said Winny with pride. "She loves music."

Christian shook his head. "Girls," he said under his breath. *Music? What does that have to do with anything?*

"Good thing for us she-gnomes, or you he-gnomes wouldn't get anything done!" Her brow furrowed, and she lightly punched his shoulder.

"Ow!"

She marched away from the chair, through the living room and into the dining room. Christian watched her. When she finally noticed he was not following her, she turned, sighed and waved him over.

"Come on. We live in here."

CHAPTER 15

Winny pulled open a door at the bottom of a gigantic wooden cabinet.

Christian, approaching slowly and asked, "Wow…isn't it dark in there?"

"No, we have light," she said, her voice edgy. They walked through the door.

"Mama, I'm back," she called loudly.

Mrs. Beezley bustled out of an old square basket that lay upon its side, wiping her hands on a white apron that covered a multi-colored patchwork dress.

"Wow!" said Christian as Mrs. Beezley smiled at him. "This is a huge home! It's so much bigger than our house." He craned his neck to see the top.

"Well, hello there, young gnome," she said,

looking around her home. "Yes, we are grateful for our luck. The Olsons never use this cabinet, so we're fairly safe in here..." She turned back to him. "...And who might you be?" She held out her hand to him, lifting an eyebrow in question.

Christian grasped it and stood tall, clasping his bag and canteen straps before answering.

"I'm Christian Tompta. I came from next door, uh, the Anderson house? My parents sent me to deliver a message." He smiled widely and threw up his arms. "It's my gnomely mission."

Mrs. Beezley and Winny both looked at Christian blankly. He stared back at them.

They said together, "Well?"

Christian faltered a moment, because he realized they were not impressed by his journey, but that they were waiting for the message. He took a deep breath.

"My father told me to tell you, 'Mr. Beezley's shoes aren't working. You need to contact Pith on his behalf and tell them he's staying at the...the...the White Truffle Inn.'"

"Oh, thorny bushes!" said Mrs. Beezley. "I wonder what's happened..." She quickly untied her apron and threw it over the back of a chair.

Winny looked unhappily at Christian, and then turned to follow her mother. Christian shuffled his feet, not knowing what else to do.

Mrs. Beezley held up a hand to her daughter. Winny stopped.

Mrs. Beezley removed her glittering blue conical hat, pressed the points of her sparkling blue shoes together, and then added the point of the hat. The air shimmered and Mrs. Beezley disappeared.

Christian's mouth dropped open.

Winny sighed. "Come on. And close your mouth," she said, turning back and guiding Christian to a pink plastic chair at a large table. "Sit down."

She busied herself fetching him a drink and a snack. He studied the room. This dining table was different from his table at home. He lifted the dark red cloth with small designs that covered it, to see the table was made from a used human butter container. Spaces were cut out for gnome legs to fit underneath. *The chairs look like human toys.*

Christian examined the kitchen accessories - gnome-sized plastic plates, cups and silverware. All of a sudden, Christian recognized the furniture. It was exactly like the toys that Hope, Zach's little sister, had played with when she was younger. *Wow. I guess it's possible to find smaller furniture, instead of using magic.*

Turning back to watch Winny, Christian sat quietly as she laid out the food. He wondered where Mrs. Beezley had gone and what she was doing.

He drank dandelion tea and ate three cilantro cookies from the plate that she set in front of him. He pretended to take great interest in the cookies, though he watched Winny from under droopy eyelashes.

She picked up her cup to take a sip of tea, but put it back down, lost in thought, without taking a drink. She paced back and forth several times, and then she stopped, took a sip of tea, and began walking laps around the table, wringing her hands. She kept glancing back toward the entrance, watching for her mother. Eventually she sat down, but then got up again to resume pacing. *I hope Mrs. Beezley gets back soon. I want to ask her about Geist and Pith and how it feels to disappear.*

"What do you think happened?" she asked. "Did your father give you any kind of clue?"

"No," he said. "Mr. Adler, the gnome from the neighbors on the other side of our house, came to our front garden and knocked on our window to bring the message. I guess the moth mixed up houses and brought it to him instead of your mother."

Winny looked at him and nodded. "Oh, this is so hard. The waiting, I mean..."

All of a sudden, the air shimmered and Mrs. Beezley appeared. It felt as if she had never left.

She walked into the dining area more calmly than she had left. Her glowing conical and shoes faded.

"What happened, Mama?" asked Winny anxiously.

"Oh, your crazy father... He stepped in muck that gummed up his shoes on the way to the village, and now his shoes won't work to pass into Geist. After his deliveries in the village, he'll have to go further into the Midnight forest, rather than come home. He has to go see the Cobbler to get his shoes repaired. He won't be home for several weeks!"

"Whew," sighed Winny, rubbing at her forehead. "Mama, do you think Mr. Olson will be alright while Papa's gone?" She stepped closer to her mother.

"Mr. Olson will be fine, love," said Mrs. Beezley. She put her arms around Winny and smoothed her hair. "The Great Master made us guardians and helpers, but his human is capable of taking care of himself for a little while. Your father will come back and help him fix anything that has gone awry during his absence, if need be."

Christian watched the two women embrace and sighed. *I could sure use a hug from Mama right now. I never thought I'd miss home so much!*

"Well, I'd better get going," said Christian. He stood up to leave, forgetting the questions he wanted to ask.

"Oh, young gnomeling, why don't you stay the night here and get a fresh start in the morning? You may sleep in Mr. Beezley's bed since he's not using it. I can bake some lavender cookies and send them with you for your trip back, too."

Mmmm... One of my favorites. Sleeping here in a bed is a good idea. I don't want to blow another good idea like I did when bunny stayed sleeping late.

He nodded. "Okay. Thank you, Mrs. Beezley."

***

Later, while Mrs. Beezley baked and then cleaned up the kitchen, Christian lay in bed unable to sleep because of thoughts that ran wildly through his head. The beds lined up against a wall in the main room, and moonlight reflected off of Winny's sleeping face.

He decided to draw her, so he sat up to dig out his dye-stick and a fresh daisy petal. Mrs. Beezley caught his eye and winked at him. His face grew warm, but then she looked away, so he began to draw. *I want to remember her, just like this.*

He was almost finished when Winny snorted and rolled over.

Christian giggled, and then he put the supplies back in his bag, carefully packing the new drawing with his others. He looked back at her once more. *I drew a pretty good likeness of her.*

He set his bag back down on the floor, and then he lay down and hummed himself to sleep.

CHAPTER 16

Christian felt a prickling sensation as he awoke from a sound sleep. He lay with his eyes closed recounting the excitement, fear, relief, cold, hunger, happiness, and homesickness of the past few days. They had taken their toll and he was grateful for a proper bed. He snuggled deeper into the blankets, but the prickling sensation grew.

Groggily, he rubbed his eyes and sat up. Both Winny and Mrs. Beezley stood over him, staring. Winny pointed and giggled at his drool-covered and rumpled appearance.

Wiping a hand across his face, he noticed they were both fresh-faced and clean as they smiled at him.

"Don't laugh, child," said Mrs. Beezley, patting

her daughter's arm. "I'm sorry to wake you this way, Christian, but the sun's coming up and it's probably better if you get started. The humans are still asleep in their beds."

Embarrassed and a little dazed, Christian patted his curly hair, which stuck straight up in several places. When it would not cooperate by laying flat, he plucked his beanie from the bedside table and yanked it over the unruly hair, pulling it down past his ears. Not wanting to dally, he stood up, adjusted his crinkled clothes, and checked his supplies.

"Yes, Ma'am."

"I've some porridge and a bean on the table for you," said Mrs. Beezley, "and I've filled your canteen and wrapped up some cookies. The weather is clear, but it's getting colder today. I've laid out an extra blanket that you may take for your journey home."

"Thank you, Mrs. Beezley," said Christian, dipping his head respectfully. Speaking came with difficulty because his mouth felt like it was full of cotton. He had not brushed his teeth through the whole trip and he needed to badly. "Could I trouble you for one more thing?"

"Of course, dear, what is it?" Both she and

Winny put hands over their noses.

"Would you happen to have an extra toothbrush?" he asked, his face growing red again under Winny's watchful eyes.

"Oh, my feathers! Of course I do. I don't know why I didn't think of that!" She winked at her daughter, who looked wide-eyed back at her and shrugged.

Christian brushed his teeth and washed his hands and face. He then used a cloth and the remaining water from the pitcher to wipe down his bag. It was covered in gunk: grass, mud, frog slime and dog saliva. The bag did not come completely clean, but it looked and smelled much better.

He noticed another odd odor and bent his head to smell his shirt. He wrinkled his nose. *Since I used up all the clean water, I'll have to find somewhere outside the house to wash. Maybe that pond... or maybe that's what caused the odor in the first place. Hmm... I'll figure out something.*

Christian quickly ate the breakfast laid out for him, and then stood up and put on his coat, canteen and bag. He packed the cookies and blanket, noticing the extra bulk.

"Thank you very much, Mrs. Beezley, for all that

you've done for me." He bowed formally at her. "I hope to repay the favor someday."

"Oh my dear..." She shook her head. "You already have - when you brought me the message!"

She waved good-bye as he left the basket with Winny.

Winny walked Christian to a doggy flap in the front door. She had been quiet the entire morning, but at the door she finally broke her silence. She stood tall and held out her hand. "Well, here it is..."

Christian nodded.

"Um...Winny?"

"Hmm?"

"Why didn't we come in this way?"

Winny laughed and shook her head.

"Oh, Christian..."

Christian suddenly did not want to leave, as he looked at the girl with the white hair and bright blue eyes.

He knew he had to go home. His parents would be worried and watching for him. He also wanted his conical hat and mystical shoes. He drew himself up tall, held out a hand and said formally, "Good-bye, Winola. It has been good meeting you. Thank you for your help."

"Good-bye, Christian." She put up a hand with her first two fingers pointing upwards and waited.

"What are you doing?" he asked. His brow wrinkled as he stared at the fingers.

Her eyes grew round as she looked at him. She wagged her fingers closer to his face.

He asked again, "What? What are you doing?" He lifted his hand and mimicked her.

Winny let out a big sigh and said, "Giving you the official gnome greeting and farewell, what do you think?"

"Um... I don't know it." He dropped his hand and looked at the floor in embarrassment, shuffling a foot.

"Just match your fingers to mine, silly," she said, exasperated. She pulled at his wrist and moved his fingers into position. Then she held his wrist in her left hand and touched her first two right fingers to his first two fingers.

Winny's face grew red, and Christian could feel his own heating up.

She dropped his wrist.

Christian chuckled, uncomfortable. "Hey, maybe your sagey-ness is coming out. Have you used that gesture before?" Christian asked.

Wrinkling her forehead, Winny said, "No, I don't think I have." Then she laughed. "Maybe I am getting sagey."

Christian shuffled his feet again. He sidestepped to the door. "Well, I'd better go."

"Yes, well, it was good to meet you," said Winny. Her face shined pink and her eyes sparkled again.

Christian gulped and cleared his throat. "It was nice to meet you too. Maybe I'll see you again."

"Yeah, maybe..." She gave a small wave.

Christian climbed through the doggy door.

He turned back once to look through the clear plastic and thought he saw a tear slip down Winny's face. *That can't be. Girls!*

Then he took his first step toward home.

A GUIDE TO MAMA T'S ACCENT

- w = v sound
- a hard th = d sound
- a soft th = t sound
- your/for = yer/fer
- the = da
- to = ta (including today, tomorrow, tonight)
- you = ya
- you're = ya're
- you'ld = ya'd

ABOUT THE AUTHOR

Dawn Paul lives in Ohio with her husband, daughter, and gnomes. She loves to write poems, short stories, and long stories. Sometimes unaccountable noises happen in her house as she's writing. She used to grow frightened, but then she realized it was just the gnomes being active and helpful.

The next book in "The Tales of Christian Tompta" series, "Home," is due out in the autumn of 2017.

With parents' or guardian's permission, visit www.ChristianTompta.com for information and fun activities!

Also with your parents' permission, you may ask questions or send comments to her on Facebook at DM Paul, on Twitter @DMPPaul or on her website at www.DMPaul.com

Thank you for purchasing this book and spending time with Christian Tompta!